"You'll be okay, F

Danny took a step closer. He looked down at her pale fingers in his hand, and he longed to lift them to his lips. He was supposed to be over her...

"Are we okay?" Beth asked, looking up at him. She was close enough that he could have bent down and caught those pink lips with his.

"You mean, are we friends?" he asked, his voice catching. He missed her so much it hurt.

She'd walked out on him, broken his heart. She'd been wrong, but that didn't change the way he still yearned for her.

Dear Reader,

This book revolves around a little boy named Luke whose heart has been broken. He wants a mom—someone to love him and protect him, to be proud of him. And my heroine is the perfect choice, if only she can sort out her issues with his father.

In my real life, my days revolve around my own little boy, who is about the same age as Luke. One day, I was walking my son's friends home from school as a favor to their mother, and another friend of mine (a mom of a little girl) saw me heading off with this group of sweet, rambunctious boys. She looked rather panicked on my behalf. The thought of caring for *that many* boys was intimidating to her. But I have a son, so little boys make sense to me. They can be complicated, but they are so worth the work! When I needed to choose a child for my hero, I knew it had to be a boy, because I just had to share that feeling when a pair of arms wrap around your neck and a little boy says, "I love you, Mom!"

If you enjoyed this book, you may enjoy my other books, too. I have two other Heartwarming releases before this one, but I also write for the Western Romance and Love Inspired lines here at Harlequin. All of my stories are sweet, which means the relationship develops without going beyond a kiss. So you can trust my books, regardless of the line they are published under.

If you'd like to connect with me, you can find me at my website, www.patriciajohnsromance.com, or on Facebook. I'd love to meet you.

Patricia

HEARTWARMING

A Boy's Christmas Wish

——

Patricia Johns

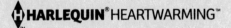

HARLEQUIN® HEARTWARMING™

Recycling programs
for this product may
not exist in your area.

ISBN-13: 978-0-373-36859-4

A Boy's Christmas Wish

Copyright © 2017 by Patricia Johns

HARLEQUIN®
www.Harlequin.com

Printed in U.S.A.

Patricia Johns writes from Alberta, Canada. She has her Hon. BA in English literature and currently writes for Harlequin's Love Inspired, Western Romance and Heartwarming lines. You can find her at patriciajohnsromance.com.

Books by Patricia Johns

Harlequin Heartwarming

A Baxter's Redemption
The Runaway Bride

Harlequin Western Romance

Hope, Montana

Safe in the Lawman's Arms
Her Stubborn Cowboy
The Cowboy's Christmas Bride
The Cowboy's Valentine Bride
The Triplets' Cowboy Daddy
Her Cowboy Boss

Harlequin Love Inspired

Comfort Creek Lawmen

Deputy Daddy

His Unexpected Family
The Rancher's City Girl
A Firefighter's Promise
The Lawman's Surprise Family

Visit the Author Profile page at Harlequin.com for more titles.

To my husband and our little boy.
You've had me by the heartstrings
from the start. I love you!

CHAPTER ONE

BETH THOMAS'S FATHER, Rick, didn't seem terribly concerned that Granny was missing. He looked up from a basket of laundry he'd been halfheartedly folding and shrugged.

"She's probably wandered off again," he said. He was a short man with a full head of iron gray hair and bushy black eyebrows, and he was staring down at the laundry as if he'd rather murder it. He was recently divorced from Beth's stepmom, Linda, and the housework seemed to irritate him more than the divorce settlement. He was a moderately successful literary novelist, and Beth was still waiting for him to inject all this unprocessed emotion into a new manuscript. So far—nada.

"Does she wander off often?" Beth asked.

"From time to time…yes."

Beth rubbed a hand over her expanding belly, and the baby wriggled inside her. She was eight months pregnant with sore feet, and Granny had been the buffer zone between Beth and her father since she'd arrived home for the holidays.

"Where does Granny go?" Beth pressed.

"The store."

For the Thomas family, "the store" never referred to the grocery store or the hardware store. Rick raised his eyes to meet her gaze, and she could see the pain there. Before Linda left, Rick had declared bankruptcy, and the corner store that had belonged to the family for three generations had been put up for sale by the bank. So much for second mortgages.

"I'll go check there," she said.

"I can do it—" Rick dropped a T-shirt back into the basket. "You should probably put your feet up or something, kiddo."

Kiddo. She was thirty-two.

"No, I'm fine, Dad. I'm supposed to get exercise anyway. I'll go see if I can find her."

Beth wanted out of the house, away from her father's irritable household chores and the stuffy smells of toast and pine-scented air freshener. She'd come home because she didn't have much choice. Her city job as a caregiver for an elderly lady had come to an end when the woman moved to a long-term care facility, and Beth was due to give birth within four short weeks. The baby's father was out of the picture, hence her return home. But her dad's divorce and bankruptcy meant that her arrival wasn't terribly convenient for him, and she could feel his frustration. He needed space, and so did she.

Beth headed down the stairs, stepping carefully. She couldn't see past her belly, and her center of gravity was off now that she was all tummy, but she made it down, shoved her feet into her boots and grabbed her cream woolen coat. It didn't close properly, but she did up the top few buttons and wrapped a scarf around her neck. It would have to do. The corner store wasn't far from her dad's house, and she angled her steps in that direction, keeping her eyes peeled for Granny.

North Fork, Alberta, was a small community on the Canadian prairies with a downtown that consisted of about four criss-crossing streets and a park next to a towering brick church. All winter long, that park had trees decorated for Christmas—an intricate design of twinkling lights that encircled a running track that was flooded to make a skating rink. She'd grown up in this town, learned to skate on that outdoor rink, and she'd even gotten engaged one Christmas in the glow of those Christmas lights to a rugged guy named Danny Brockwood, who'd come to town for a job as a millwright.

But that had been five years ago, and that engagement had ended in heartbreak when she discovered he'd been lying to her the entire time—he had a child that he'd never told her about. So she packed up and went to the city, where she'd hoped for a fresh start. A degree in medieval studies qualified her for absolutely nothing in particular, and she'd gotten a job with a private company caring for the elderly in their homes. Sometimes, when she got home from work and flung herself on her couch, she'd look at the blank TV and wonder how Danny was doing. It was her own bad luck to have fallen in love with the wrong guy.

Beth stopped at an intersection and looked both ways, scanning for the familiar form of a slender old lady in a bright red jacket and clomping winter boots. Alberta was cold and dry this time of year, the snow swirling into banks on the sides of the street—not even needing salt to melt it off the asphalt. The wind blew in powerful gusts, stopped only by the low houses. The prairies had no other wind blocks, just section upon section of frozen farmland, bared to elements. However, for all the arctic winds, the sun shone bright and cheery. Beth had often wondered how people used to endure this kind of cold before electricity and water heaters.

Granny might run off, but apparently, she was with it enough to put on a coat and boots before she did. Perhaps that was why her dad didn't worry quite so much. Besides, in a town the size of North Fork, everyone knew everyone, and someone was bound to bring her home again. Granny was a fixture around here—the lady from the corner store. What kid didn't know her? And what adult hadn't bought tiny paper bags of bulk candy from her in their own childhoods?

The corner store was just ahead, and Beth plodded toward it. It was closed down now, the windows papered over and the neon signs that used to flicker in the windows gone. Her heart constricted at the sight of it. That store had been her home just as much as the house, or the town; it had been her respite from her by-the-book stepmother.

Beth waited for a truck to pass, and she tugged her coat a little closer around her belly. The cold was seeping into her fingers and toes, and while pregnancy had left her generally overheated, a coat she couldn't zip certainly took care of that. She crossed the road and stopped again, looking in all directions. No sign of Granny.

"Granny!" Shouting in the middle of the road didn't seem to do much good, either, since the only response was the bark of a dog from a nearby yard.

Beth stopped in front of the store and looked up, her gaze focusing on the For Sale sign. Except it wasn't for sale anymore... there was a big banner covering it stating Sold.

She sighed. It was to be expected, of course, but it still hurt. Someone had snapped it up, and soon enough that old store would be turned into something else. A Laundromat or a coffee shop. Whatever business ended up there, the Thomas family wouldn't have the heart to frequent it.

The door was ajar, and Beth gave it a pull. It opened with that familiar jingle of the bell overhead, and she stepped inside. Nothing had changed. The old shelves were still in the same place, except most of the product was gone. There was one shelf that still held various odds and ends that looked fully stocked. She heaved a sigh.

"Hey."

Beth startled as a man stood up from behind one of those shelves, his hands full of cardboard, and she caught her breath when she recognized him. He was tall and dark, as he always had been, but the last five years had solidified him. He stared at her in equal surprise, and he dropped the cardboard and brushed his hands off, then came around the shelf.

"Danny…" she breathed. "What are you doing here?"

She swallowed hard and tugged at her jacket again, as if by covering her belly she could protect herself from that barrage of emotion.

"What are *you* doing here?" he countered.

"I was looking for Granny. And I just wanted to stop in and see the old place before it—" She didn't finish that thought. What was Danny Brockwood doing here? Did he know the new owner or something?

"I haven't seen her," he said. "You... um—" His gaze moved down to her belly, then up to her face again. "You look good."

"Thanks." She wouldn't address it. Yes, she was pregnant, but Danny didn't get explanations. He didn't deserve them. He could just stand there and wonder.

"How are you doing?" he asked. "I thought you'd have come back to town before this."

"I was busy." That's what people said, wasn't it? At least people who wanted to save face. "How is your son?"

Danny pulled a hand through his hair, but something in his expression softened in a way she'd never seen before. "He's eight now. Almost nine. He's a good kid. Smart as a whip, too."

Luke was the secret that Danny had kept from Beth until five days before their wedding. Then his ex-girlfriend dropped his toddler son on his doorstep and told him that it was his turn at parenting. That was a big secret to have kept from her. People didn't have children and then just forget—it had been a willful omission, and if he could hide something that big, what else could he hide? Her faith in her swarthy fiancé's love had shriveled. This wasn't about romance anymore; it was about real-life challenges and her ability to take him at his word. But her fears went deeper than that. She'd seen the way he looked at that little boy, and she recognized that they shared a connection she never would. She'd had a stepmother of her own, and she wasn't keen on taking on that role for herself.

"So, are you married?" Danny asked after a beat of silence.

"No." She tugged at her coat again. "Single." She wasn't going to pretend that things were any different than they were. She was very much on her own in this.

"When are you due?" he asked.

He eyed her in that curious way he used to do when they were younger and dating, and she felt a small part of her resentful heart thaw.

"It's rude to ask about a pregnancy that hasn't been confirmed yet, you know," she said wryly, and Dànny cracked a grin.

"Hard to deny that one, Beth."

"I'm due January fourth," she said, smoothing a hand over her stomach. "And it's a girl."

Danny nodded slowly. "Congratulations. You really do look beautiful."

Everyone had to say that to a pregnant woman—she knew that. She felt puffy now, and huge.

"So what *are* you doing here?" Beth asked, glancing around. "I noticed that the store is sold."

"I bought it." His gaze didn't even flicker as he said it. "It was a price I couldn't refuse."

Her heart sank. This was adding insult to injury. She'd never fully recovered from calling off their wedding, and now when her family was going through their hardest times since, Danny was the one to swoop in and buy up their heritage?

"You?" She stared at him, aghast. "*You* bought our store?"

The bell above the door jingled behind her, and Beth turned to see Granny step inside. Her coat was open in the front, and the old lady smiled sweetly when she saw Beth and Danny.

"You two lovebirds," Granny said with a low laugh. "Don't block customers now."

Granny wasn't completely with them, it would seem. Her mind was firmly fixed in the past. She headed over to the shelf that still held some dusty bags of sunflower seeds and assorted items like windshield scrapers and expired lip balm.

"These prices," she tutted. "Far too high. Nothing will sell at this price…"

And ironically, Granny might be right. None of that product had ever sold.

DAN COULDN'T HELP but steal another glance at Beth. She had always been gorgeous, but pregnancy had brought out a glow in her that he'd never seen before. Her golden hair tumbled around her shoulders in glossy curls, and her lips were fuller with the extra weight she carried. Her belly was like a perfect dome out in front of her. She seemed softer, somehow, and more vulnerable. And if the twenty-seven-year-old, trim-waisted Beth had been enough to fire his blood back then, this more mature version of the same woman, rounder and fuller, just about stopped his heart.

Except he knew better than to entertain those thoughts. Beth had dumped him because she couldn't handle being a stepmother. Obviously, he should have told her about his son sooner, but until Lana had shown up on his doorstep, he hadn't known that he would ever be allowed into his son's life. Regardless, Beth had walked out because she didn't want to be stepmom to his child, which he'd understood back then. He'd lied to her, and if there was one thing Beth could not abide, it was an untruth, and knowing that should have been enough to make him come clean. Except that was a part of his life he hadn't been proud of—being the deadbeat dad of a kid he'd never met. It wasn't that he'd been trying to hide anything from her—Lana had made it clear that she wanted nothing to do with him when they broke up before he moved to North Fork. He'd tried to contact Lana a few times afterward, and he'd gotten nothing but silence.

"Someone had to buy the place," Dan said, and Beth's attention whipped away from her grandmother and back to him. Her eyes glittered.

"You never liked my dad." He could hear

the accusation in her tone. What did she think, that he'd done this as some sort of revenge plot because Rick Thomas hadn't thought he was good enough for Beth?

"Your dad never liked *me*," he retorted. "And this has nothing to do with old tensions. I think we're pretty much past all that, don't you?"

Her dad had been right. Dan *hadn't* been good enough for Beth. He'd come to North Fork for work—the oil fields about three hours north providing a lot of employment opportunities for large-equipment mechanics. When he'd seen Beth around town, he'd been drawn in by her effortless charm. She came from a respected family—her father being the Rick Thomas of literary fame— and she'd gone to University of Alberta for a degree, something that felt wildly out of reach for a guy like him. He'd never been terribly scholarly. He was a skilled worker and he loved his trade, but she had a way of talking that exposed a world he knew little about—a world with books and theories, history and primary sources. Her dad had written weighty masterpieces that were studied in Canadian literature classes the country over. There were three of them, and a fourth that he'd been working on for the last decade.

Beth sighed. "So what are you going to do with this place?"

"I'm going to open a tool shop," Dan said. "A lot of guys in the trades have to drive into the city to get their tools, and it's a waste of fuel and annoying to boot. I want to open a tool shop that carries most of the basics. I'll order in the specialty tools on demand—"

Beth was staring at him, tears misting her eyes. Shoot. Okay, maybe she hadn't wanted to hear his business plan, but what did she expect him to do with the place?

"I can't keep it a corner store," Dan qualified.

"I know." She sucked in a breath.

"And the price was shockingly low—"

Beth shot him another pained glance, and he kicked himself. He wasn't trying to hurt her here, but when the store had come up for sale at that price, the timing had been perfect. He'd been selling tools out of his garage for months, and he was making a pretty good profit. There was a demand for tools in this town, and this could be his first retail space. Lucky for him the bank agreed.

"I'm sorry about your dad," Dan said, softening his tone. "I know he worked hard to build the business, and losing it all like that is horrible. I feel for him."

She didn't answer at first, and then she rubbed a hand over her stomach. "Well, he's had more than one big shock in the last few months."

"Linda leaving," Dan clarified. That divorce had taken North Fork by surprise.

"Oh, no. They planned it out so they could separate 'amicably.'" She did finger quotes around the last word. "Dad says it was coming for a while. Linda's nothing if not detail oriented. I was referring to me."

"The baby," he confirmed.

"He worries a lot," she said. "And he's got a lot going on right now, so the timing could have been better."

"So how's your brother?" Dan asked.

"Perfectly successful in Illinois, thanks," she replied with a wry smile.

Her older brother was a professor at a state college—the bar had been set quite high for the Thomas family. He could sympathize with Beth's position right now. She'd deserved better than being left on her own for the biggest challenge of her life.

"Don't know if this is rude to ask, but who's the dad?"

"None of your business," she retorted with a cool smile, and Dan laughed.

"You haven't changed a bit," he said.

She smiled and rolled her eyes. "You'd be surprised, Danny."

Danny...he hadn't been called that in a long time.

"Look." He cleared his throat. "If you see anything that you want in here...I bought the whole place, contents included. But I don't need any of it—" He was doing it again, minimizing a lifetime of Thomas family memories in this old place, which wasn't his intent. "What I mean to say is, if there is anything that you want from the store, it's yours. I only got the keys today, so I'm looking at everything for the first time, too."

"Thank you." She nodded. "There will be things. Like the bell over the door."

"Yeah, yeah." He nodded. "Take it." He glanced up and realized it was high over her head, and in her current state a stepladder would be a bad idea. "Or I can get it down for you."

He caught her eye, and he felt a swell of sympathy. Things had been hard for the Thomas family lately, and he was just an added insult.

Beth was beautiful and smart, with a sharp sense of humor. He'd always imagined that she'd gone to Edmonton and met some bookish type who would be impressed by her father's name. Then she'd get married and drive a quality SUV, have some beautiful babies… She was making good on that last one, and for that he was grudgingly glad.

Parenthood had a way of improving a person. It carved them out and deepened them. It took a heart and stretched it farther than a person thought possible. It changed weekend plans from drinks or watching the game into cartoon movies and playing in the snow. Luke's arrival had been a shock, but he'd changed Dan's life for the better in every way possible. Dan had always hoped that he'd be a successful business owner here in town, and that when people saw him coming they'd call him "Mr. Brockwood." Turned out that his deepest satisfaction came from being called "Dad."

He glanced at his watch. Luke would be out of school soon.

"So how is your grandmother doing?" he asked.

They both instinctively looked over to where Granny was arranging the shelf, wiping dust off the packages with her palm.

"Not so good," Beth said softly. "She keeps slipping into the past. And apparently, she's been wandering off a lot."

"I noticed that," he agreed. He'd driven her home a couple of times when he'd found her on the street looking confused.

"And she keeps asking about Grandpa." Beth's eyes glittered with emotion.

"What do you do?" he asked.

"We tell her that he's gone out for milk," Beth said with a shrug. "It sure beats breaking her heart fourteen times a day telling her that he died. So if she ever asks—"

"Yeah, right. Milk…" He nodded.

Everyone loved Beth's grandmother, whom most people called Granny. She was that sort of lady. And when Beth had agreed to marry him, when a furious Rick had kept encouraging his daughter to think this through a little more, Granny had been happy for them. Dan would never forget that. She'd taken his hand in hers and smiled up into his eyes and said, "Marriage is a blessing, Danny. May you two be brilliantly happy." For a guy who'd grown up with minimal encouragement, her words had meant the world.

"Granny, we should go," Beth called. "We need to get back."

"No, I'd better mind the store," Granny said with a decisive shake of her head. "It's too early to close."

Beth and Dan exchanged a glance.

"Danny will mind the shop, Granny," Beth said. "Right, Danny?"

"Yeah, of course," Dan said. "Don't worry, Granny, I'll take care of everything."

Granny brushed her hands off and came back toward them. "Are you sure, Danny?"

"I'm sure," he said earnestly.

"Do you know how to use the cash register?" she pressed.

"Yes, ma'am. Beth showed me."

Granny didn't look convinced, but eventually she smiled. "Well, you are going to be part of the family very soon, aren't you?

I think it's only right that we trust you with a few responsibilities."

In Granny's mind, Dan and Beth were still engaged, he realized, and his throat suddenly felt tight. Of all the days to go back to, those were happy ones. Too happy to last, but happy.

Granny smoothed her hands over her jacket.

"Can I help you zip up?" Beth asked.

"Oh, my…" Granny's eyes grew large as she focused on Beth's round belly. "Look at you!"

Granny glanced back at Danny with a look of shock, and he was forced to hide a smile. Yeah, there'd been a time when he'd have loved to take the credit for Beth's glowing pregnancy, but not now.

"Okay, let's just go," Beth said hurriedly.

"The sooner the better on that wedding, my dear," Granny said pointedly, and Beth shot Danny a look of exasperation.

"Beth, I'm cleaning this place out over the next couple of weeks. Come by and take anything you want," Dan said.

"Thank you," Beth said. "I'll come by tomorrow, if that's okay."

"Not a problem. I'll be here."

Beth pushed the door open, and she and her grandmother left the store, the soft ding of the bell echoing in the stillness as the door swung shut again.

Beth Thomas was back, and Dan wasn't sure how he felt about that. All those old memories—all those old feelings—came in a flood. But fatherhood had changed everything for Dan, and there was no going back.

CHAPTER TWO

"DANNY BROCKWOOD?" Rick exploded. "That twit has my store? He never said a thing to me. How fast did that sale go through?"

Granny came inside and unzipped her coat, then proceeded into the middle of the kitchen with her snowy boots still on her feet.

"I'm not sure," Beth said, peeling off her jacket. "Granny, your boots."

"Oh…silly me…" Granny came back to the door and bent to take her boots off. She was still physically spry, and while it seemed horrible for Beth to wish such a thing, if Granny would just get a little creaky in the knees or something, she might not make it so far when she wandered off. It was worse when the mind went before the body did, because there was so much more that could go wrong.

"He said the price was too good to refuse,

so it looks like Danny had some money in the bank," Beth said, hanging her coat on a peg. "Millwrights make a good wage."

"Where is Ralph?" Granny asked as she stepped into her slippers. "Ralph!"

"He's gone for milk, Granny," Rick said. "Why don't you go get settled in the living room? Warm up."

"Oh…" Granny nodded. "Yes, that's a good idea."

They waited until Granny had retreated to her favorite recliner and the footrest popped up. Beth shot her father an apologetic look.

"I thought it would be better if you heard it from me," she said.

"It would have been better if he'd been man enough to tell me himself," Rick snapped.

"No, it wouldn't," Beth said with a sigh. "You hate everything Danny does. It would have given you a chance to yell at him, that's it."

"And that's too much to ask?" Rick muttered something under his breath. This was a personal loss for Rick—the store he'd helped his father build up. He'd set his last novel in a family-run corner store, just like theirs, and the critics had deemed it "important" and "layered." They'd said they could feel the "regional heartbeat" in his work.

"Dad, I hate this, too," she admitted. "Our family used to be respected."

"We *are* respected. Hard times don't change that."

He had a point, but this wasn't what any of them had expected. If the town were to place bets on which of them would hit bottom, they'd have all put their money on Danny to slide down into ruin. Not the Thomases. But her father wasn't the man he used to be since Linda had left, and Beth hadn't decided if that was a good thing or not. That was ironic, considering how much she'd disliked her stepmother. They'd never gotten along, not that Linda was entirely to blame. Beth hadn't been easy on her.

"Have you met his son?" Beth asked after a moment.

"You mean Danny's son?" Rick asked. "Yeah, I've seen him around. Luke's a good kid."

She nodded. "Funny to think of Danny as a father."

"Funny to think of my little girl as a

mother," her father retorted. "Some of these things creep up on a person."

"Har har." She cast her father an annoyed look. When was he going to stop being scandalized over this? She was due in a month. He'd had time to get used to the idea.

"And speaking of parenthood," her father said, "we need to talk about getting child support."

"No."

"Even Luke's mother came after Danny to do his part," Rick said with a shake of his head.

"She wouldn't let him near the kid before she dumped him on his doorstep," she countered.

"Fine. Whatever. My point is, babies don't come into the world by accident. It takes a cooperative act between two people, and it isn't right for the full financial burden to fall on only one of them."

"Dad, I'm not going after child support."

What was she supposed to do, try to track down some random Australian tourist who'd happened to drink in a certain bar in Edmonton one spring night after her boyfriend had dumped her? It wasn't even a possibility, but this wasn't a story she could tell her father. She'd kept her mouth shut until now, and she was keeping it that way.

"It's Collin's baby, isn't it?" her father pressed. "I mean, obviously it is. I'm not stupid."

Collin was the accountant she'd been dating in Edmonton until he'd broken up with her. He was taking a job across the country in the Maritimes, and he didn't feel their relationship would last long distance. He hadn't mentioned her going with him, either. But he wasn't the father.

Her father scrubbed a hand through his gray hair. "Beth, the book royalties have been a trickle at best. I'm not in a position—"

"I know," she said quietly.

"I told Linda she could have the investments and the car. She was the mind behind the investments anyway. I just wanted to keep my shop and this house. I can always write more books."

On the surface, it sounded like her father had come out ahead in the settlement, except for the fact that the store had been on the brink of bankruptcy and the house wasn't worth much in a town this size. If they put it on the market, it would be nearly impossible to sell. No one moved to North Fork. People moved out.

"Dad, I'm not asking for anything."

"You might not be asking," he retorted. "But the reality is that kids are expensive. You're going to have day care, food, diapers. And just wait until this kid starts school! School supplies, school clothes…"

Beth knew all of this, which was why she'd come home. But she was a burden around here. Coming home wasn't the problem—it was coming home pregnant.

"After the baby is old enough, I'll go back to work," Beth said.

"See, this is the thing." Her father's voice grew gruff. "I want you have a choice. I don't want you pushed into a corner."

"But I don't have a choice!" she countered.

"You could have more of a choice if you made the father of this baby take some responsibility," he said.

They could argue this in circles all night, and they'd still never agree, because her dad was convinced that Collin was the father, and if that were so, Collin had a job and a stable income. He could easily pay child support.

"I know you think Collin is the father, but he isn't."

"He isn't." Her father eyed her critically. "Who is?"

"I'm not telling you that."

"You have to think of your baby," he said.

"Do you think I *don't*?" Tears misted her eyes. "I think of very little else, Dad!"

In four short weeks, give or take, Beth was going to be the mother of a baby girl, and she'd be responsible for this little person's well-being for the rest of her life. She could feel her daughter move and stretch inside her, and when she lay in bed at night, she'd play games with her by pressing on her belly and feeling the baby tap back. She'd already named her: Riley Elinor. Elinor since that was Granny's first name, and Riley because Beth liked it. No other reason than that, and there wasn't a father to debate with over names.

"Linda would have known how to handle this," her father said with a sigh.

"Linda was a cold, brittle witch, Dad!"

"Say what you like about her, she was

here!" her father snapped. "At least I gave you a stepmother to help with all the girly things I knew nothing about!"

Beth pressed her lips together. This was not the time for this argument. Her father had married Linda about a year after Beth's mother passed away from cancer. Beth had been twelve, and she'd hated the idea of her father loving another woman from the very start. So, granted, they hadn't had the smoothest of transitions, but Linda had been a chilly and unsupportive woman. Linda knew what she expected, and she didn't waver in that: homework done on time, kitchen cleaned nightly, a half hour of TV a night and skirts to the knee. Beth realized that didn't sound horrible, but there also hadn't been any softness or understanding. Linda hadn't liked Beth very much, and she'd never hidden it well.

Beth's brother, Michael, on the other hand, had been more likable in Linda's eyes. She'd never been a doting kind of woman, and heaven knew she'd never tried to take their mother's place. But Michael got off easier on everything, and when he went on to get his PhD and a teaching position, Linda had never been prouder.

"Well, now you don't have Linda to help you figure it out," her father snapped. "And I don't have any answers, either."

"I'm glad Linda isn't here for this—" she began, but she stopped when she saw Granny standing in the doorway. The old woman's eyes filled with angry tears.

"Granny," Beth said, softening her tone.

"Now listen here, both of you." Granny's expression was like lightning. "Beth is pregnant. That's true. There is no going back and undoing that, but I see no use fighting over it!"

"I know, Mom," Rick said. "I'm sorry. We'll keep it down."

Was Granny back in the present? It was an emotional relief when Granny's mind cleared for a few minutes.

"And for crying out loud," Granny added, "she's getting married in a few months! She's marrying the father of her child, and while in my day we hid that kind of thing a little more effectively, I don't see what the big deal is now!"

No, Granny was stuck in the past again, and Beth pulled a hand through her hair.

"I'm going to tell you something, Ricky," Granny went on. "I was three months pregnant with you when I married your father. We eloped, he and I, because you were on the way! It was a big deal back then, so we fudged our anniversary so you'd never know. But your dad and I have been very happy together. So stop hounding this poor girl and let her get married!"

Beth stared at her grandmother in surprise. In Granny's day, that would have been quite the scandal. To think, Granny had shared that secret to stand up for her... Except she wasn't marrying anybody, and Danny had nothing to do with her pregnancy. Still, Granny had meant well.

"I didn't know that, Mom," her father said. "Thanks for telling me."

"Are you going to give her a break already?" Granny pressed.

"Yes, of course."

Granny reached out and put a hand on Beth's arm. "You should probably get off your feet, dear."

Granny headed back into the living room,

and Beth met her father's gaze with a small smile.

"Wow," Beth said. "I'm not the only scandal around here."

Her father shook his head. "She's told me that about four times already. She keeps forgetting." Her father heaved a sigh. "I'm only looking out for you, Beth. I'm not judging you. I'm doing my best, and I feel like it isn't enough."

"I'm a grown woman, Dad," Beth replied. "I'll figure it out. You don't need to worry."

Except he would worry. She knew that. Under it all, he was still her daddy, and she had come home in the most vulnerable state possible...right when he had nothing left to give.

DAN STOOD ON a stepladder to unscrew the bell over the top of the door. It tinkled dully against his sleeve as he worked, and when the second screw finally came out of the wall, he pulled the bell free. How long had this been here?

The corner store had been a fixture in this town, and he did feel a little bit bad that he was the one to tear apart a place with so much history, but a corner store couldn't make money anymore. Especially not with the chain gas stations selling all the same product cheaper. That was why Rick had gone out of business. Dan wasn't supposed to feel guilty here, and yet somehow he did. Just a little.

He also hadn't counted on Beth coming back to town… Pregnant Beth. That had been a shock, all right. He'd thought that he'd cleared his heart of her years ago when she'd walked out on him, but seeing her again had proven him wrong. He definitely felt something, even if it was mingled with anger. He knew he'd messed up by not telling her about his son sooner, but in his defense, he'd never met the boy, and Lana seemed to have dropped off the map. Then when Lana showed up with a little boy with big brown eyes, his world had turned upside down, and he'd hoped Beth would stand by him. But she couldn't—she was betrayed by the surprise, and he was equally betrayed by her abandonment.

Yeah, he'd messed up, but so had she. Marriage was for better or for worse, and they'd been just days from the ceremony, and she'd still walked out. What about their commitment to each other? This was his *son*, and any woman who couldn't love Luke, too, didn't belong with him, much as it hurt. So whatever he still felt for her was tempered by reality.

Dan put the bell down on the front counter and glanced out the window in time to see Beth approaching. He'd told her to come and take what she wanted, and it looked like she wasn't wasting any time. He paused and watched her pick her way around icy patches. Her breath hung in the air, and as he watched her careful movements, he remembered an image he'd had in his mind a long time ago…back when he'd asked her to marry him, when he'd thought about starting a family with her and what she'd look like pregnant with their baby.

And there she was—fully, richly pregnant. He stepped away from the window so she wouldn't see him, but his heart was already beating quicker than it was before. Beth had always done this to him, mixed him up and made him yearn for more…

The front door opened, and a whoosh of cold air swept in ahead of Beth. She slammed the door shut behind her and shivered.

"It's cold out," she said.

Dan nodded toward a space heater he had humming in the center of the store. "That'll help."

She moved over to the heater and pulled off her gloves, then held her hands out.

"I took the bell down for you," he said, picking it up from the counter and bringing it to her across the room.

Beth took the bell with a wistful smile. "Grandpa hung this."

"I thought so," he admitted, then cleared his throat. "Look, my goal is to have everything cleaned out by Christmas. I want to open shop in the new year. I'll be working pretty quickly to get it all done."

"Sounds like you'd have to." She glanced around sadly.

"There are probably more things around here that you'll want, but it'll be hard for me to know what's meaningful and what isn't."

"I was thinking the same thing," she admitted. "What if I…helped?"

"I hate to break it to you, Beth," he said with a wry smile. "But you're pregnant and I'm not going to be responsible for you hurting yourself."

"Then what would you suggest?" she asked.

"You *not* helping," he said with a short laugh. "But definitely come by. I mean, you can go through the stuff I'm tearing out and make sure you've got everything you want."

"I won't be in the way?" she asked.

"Probably will be," he admitted. "But I'll survive."

"All right, then." She smiled. "Thanks."

He'd probably live to regret this, but his guilt for taking over a place that meant so much to the Thomases had been piqued. Dealing with Rick's resentment would have been one thing, but Beth's arrival back in town had softened him.

For the next hour, Beth sat on a crate and sorted through the last of the product that Rick hadn't already taken. Dan dismantled a slushie machine and carried it outside piece by piece. On his last trip to the garbage bin out back, he entered the store to find Beth behind the till. She was sorting through some drawers, and she held up a small, triple frame that held three photos—one of Rick, one of a teenage Michael and the other of Beth in her girlhood.

Dan crossed the room and took it from her fingers to look closer. Beth had been pretty then, but the beauty that would develop was still sleeping behind big teeth and crooked bangs.

"That's you, all right," he said. "You were a cute kid."

"I gave this to Linda one year for her birthday," Beth said, then shook her head. "Dad pressured me into making an effort, so I did. I thought I'd give her something that showed she was part of the family. I gave it to her here, and she didn't take it with her."

"She left it in the drawer," Dan concluded.

Beth nodded. "Dad told me later that it hadn't sent the message I thought. It was a frame with me, my brother and my dad. Linda wasn't included."

"You hated your dad marrying her, didn't you?" he asked.

Beth sighed. "I wasn't easy to deal with. I'll admit that. I didn't like her from the start because she wasn't my mother, and my mother had been wonderful. Mom loved us with her whole heart, and no one could eclipse her…"

"But your dad must have been lonely,"

Dan said. "Your mom was gone, and he was on his own with you kids."

She took the frame back from him and looked down at the faces for a moment. "You're a single dad now, too..."

"And I can appreciate how hard that is," Dan admitted. "Being a dad—it's amazing, but it's lonely. I'd never undo Luke. He's the best thing in my life, but parenthood can be isolating. You child doesn't take the place of a partner."

"I guess I'll find that out soon enough," she said.

"Yeah. It'll be the best ride of your life, hands down."

"You say your child doesn't take the place of a partner," she said. "So you must date, then." A blush rose in her cheeks. She must have realized how it sounded, and he shot her a teasing grin.

"We've done that once, Beth. Probably best if we don't do it again."

"I'm not interested in dating you," she retorted. "I'm asking because I'll be a single mom very soon, and I can't imagine trying to juggle dating and a baby."

"It's not easy," he admitted. "And no, I

don't really date. I'm busy with Luke, I'm careful about who he meets, and that doesn't leave a whole lot of time for a relationship." Her eyebrows went up, and he shot her a grin. "Didn't expect that, did you?"

"I'm not used to seeing you as a dad."

"Ditto." He smiled faintly, and she looked down at her belly.

"Oh…well, yes. I suppose we're even there, aren't we?"

Dan regarded her thoughtfully. He was curious about Rick and Linda—all of North Fork was. They were one of those established couples that everyone expected to bicker good-naturedly until they died. Rick was the quieter one, with his laptop set up on the store counter, and Linda was the go-getter. It had shocked everyone when they announced their intention to separate.

"So what happened between your dad and Linda?" Dan asked. "From the outside, there weren't any cracks."

"She left him," Beth said.

"Really." Dan sighed. "That's rough. How come? Another guy?"

"Not that we know of," Beth replied. "But Linda was always a little frustrated by Dad.

She wanted him to be the alpha male, but she didn't like being countered, either. So no matter what he did, she wasn't happy."

"Hmm." Dan nodded. "She decided to leave and your dad just went along with it?"

That was the weird part. Rick hadn't gotten soppy or angry—at least not in public. He'd just been the supportive guy he'd always been, as if they were announcing Linda was taking a job, or something. But it had been the end of their marriage.

"Dad was tired," she replied. "And I don't know…I mean, I was in the city. Whatever their relationship morphed into, I have no idea. But I do know that when Linda said she was leaving him, he was both sad and kind of relieved. I think he was just…tired."

"After so many years together," Dan said. He'd always been curious, at the very least. Not that Rick and Linda had ever been nice to him.

Beth met his gaze. "I'm not going to argue that they should have stayed married."

Neither would he. "I know Linda was hard on you."

"Kids need love, Dan. She was big on structure and manners but pretty low on affection. And while I might have been a hard kid to love, I still needed more than she gave."

Hard to love. Was that how she'd seen herself? And she might have been—he hadn't known her then, but the thought of her feeling unlovable as fragile preteen who'd just lost her mom was heartbreaking.

"You were a kid, Beth," he said. "You couldn't have been that hard to love…"

Beth turned her attention back to the drawer. "Pass me the garbage."

Dan did as she asked, and she dumped the rest of the contents of the drawer into the trash can, then replaced the drawer.

"Dad never did stand up to her," Beth went on. "He could have told her that she needed to be kinder. He could have told her to back off and let him have some time alone with me. But Linda was always there, guarding her turf as if I was competition for my dad's love."

"I agree there," Dan said quietly. "He should have stood up for you. You were his daughter, and you were the child. You needed your dad to be your champion."

Beth smiled. "Thank you. It's nice to be agreed with on that."

Dan was the kind of dad who would do just that—stick up for his son. Like Beth said, kids needed love, and if he was ever put into a position to choose between his son and a woman, his son would win. In fact, looking back on it, Beth had done him a favor by walking away. Because even if their wedding had been earlier, Luke would have still ended up on his doorstep, and Dan was glad that he'd never been put into the position to choose between his child and his wife. How had she put it? *Danny, asking me to marry you and asking me to be a stepmother to your child are two different proposals! I can't do this!*

He might not have been mature enough back then to make the right choice often enough.

CHAPTER THREE

THAT EVENING AT HOME, Beth stood in the living room, looking at the place in front of the big window where they normally put up the tree. The room was bare of Christmas cheer. She'd been home for several days now, and they still hadn't gotten around to decorating.

"We need to put the tree up, Dad."

"I'm not real festive this year, kiddo," he said.

"All the more reason for us to do it," Beth replied. "I don't feel like it, either, but I think we need this."

"I don't know…" Her father sighed.

"For me." Beth caught his eye. "I could use some Christmas cheer."

He pushed himself up from the couch. "If I drag the tree out, then you'll have to decorate. Deal?"

Rick pulled the artificial tree out of the basement, and Granny joyfully helped add the family ornaments to it. Rick was quiet, but he put a few baubles on the tree, pausing to look at the more meaningful ones like Baby's First Christmas or one of the few surviving school craft ornaments Beth or Michael had made years ago.

"Do you remember this one?" He held up a Popsicle-stick Christmas tree.

"Not really. I must have been pretty small," Beth said with a short laugh.

"Well, I remember it." He put it on one of the branches. "You came home from kindergarten with globs of glue in your hair, but you'd produced this. It was your masterpiece."

He'd have to remember for the both of them, but his retelling of the story made Beth smile. Over the years, as the glue broke apart and those school-made ornaments crumbled, Linda would toss them in the trash without a twinge of emotion.

"Linda bought this one," he said, holding up a custom ornament of a book with the cover of her father's first release. "I know she was difficult sometimes, Beth, but that woman understood me."

"Your writing, you mean," Beth clarified.

"She read every book I wrote about three times each," he said. "She could quote from them. And she knew what I needed to be productive…" He hung the ornament with a low sigh.

Her mother had respected Rick's writing, too, but she'd been a little less in awe of his abilities. Mom had kept Dad down-to-earth. Linda had admired him more, Beth had to admit. She'd always encouraged him to write, even if it meant she saw less of him. His writing had been her passion, too.

"Where's the star?" Beth asked as she got to the bottom of the box of ornaments. She looked around.

"Oh…" Her father scrubbed a hand through his gray hair. "It's up in the attic of the store."

"What?" Beth frowned. "Why?"

"I couldn't fit it in the closet without crushing it, so I tucked it up there. I figured it would last longer."

And Beth could understand that protective sentiment—it was the same star they'd used on their tree for as long as Beth could remember. Nothing exciting—plastic and tinsel. It probably used up insane amounts of electricity when they plugged it in, but it was tradition, and she was softened to realize that her father had quietly protected that star over the years. It was one thing Linda hadn't gotten her hands on.

"I'll get it tomorrow," Beth promised. "You can still drive me to my doctor's appointment, right?"

"Sure thing, kiddo," her father said with a nod.

THE NEXT DAY, the doctor was kind and thorough. Dr. Oduwale was her childhood best friend's mother, and when she was done examining her, she'd looked her in the eye earnestly and asked, "What do you need, my dear?"

"Nothing," Beth assured her. "I'm fine. I've got Dad, and we're sorting it all out. How is the baby?"

Dr. Oduwale assured her that all was well and they were simply waiting now. Well, waiting—and pretending she was more confident than she was, Beth thought… So she thanked Dr. Oduwale and tried to smile more brightly than she felt.

"Just keep your stress low and get ready

for the baby," Dr. Oduwale said. "Everything looks great. You've got to call Abby. She's missed you."

And Beth would call Abby…just not yet. She wasn't sure how much more brilliant confidence she could pull off without cracking.

As Beth walked to the store later that day, she felt more optimistic—and this time it wasn't an act. Maybe there had been more going on behind the scenes between her father and Linda than she'd ever noticed. Maybe she wasn't quite as alone as she'd thought if her father had been guarding something as precious and fragile as a twenty-year-old Christmas star all these years by storing it in the one place Linda would never venture…

Deeper down, Beth saw something uncomfortable to acknowledge—unfair, even. Linda's Christmases had all been spent around an artificial tree with memories attached to it that predated her. She'd bought some new ornaments every year—mostly representing things that mattered between her and Rick—and she'd put them on the tree in a prominent place. Beth had resented that attempt to insert herself, but then, Beth had resented almost anything her stepmother had done. Seeing her father look at that custom-made ornament of his book, she realized that Linda's Christmases wouldn't have been ideal. Beth wasn't proud of that, especially now. A little bit of charity wouldn't have killed her.

Beth found the door to the corner store unlocked, and she pulled it open and stepped inside. The warm air was welcome, and she rubbed her gloved hands together. Danny was sweeping out the corners where refrigerators used to stand. His sleeves were rolled up to reveal muscular forearms. He looked up as she came inside.

"Hi," she said.

"Hey." A smile crept across his face. "Cold?"

She nodded and pulled off her gloves, setting them on the counter. "It's not too bad out there, though. Feels warmer than yesterday." She headed toward the heater and unwound her scarf.

"Yeah, I thought the same thing. There's no wind today—that's the difference."

"Must be…" Like everyone else in this

town, they knew how to make small talk about weather. But Beth had more on her mind than the windchill. "Can I ask you something?" she asked.

"Sure."

"How horrible was I to Linda?"

"When I knew you?" he asked.

"Yeah."

Danny grimaced. "She had a lot of it coming."

That was answer enough. "So I was bad." Even as an adult.

"You reacted," he said. "Can't really blame you for that. She pushed your buttons a lot."

Still, Beth wished she had a little less to regret.

"I think it takes a special sort of person to raise someone else's kid," she said with a sigh. "Like a saint. I wasn't fun when I was a kid. Maybe not even after I was grown."

"You said you didn't want to be a stepmother," Danny said. "When Lana dropped Luke off—"

"It was a shock," she said. "You'd never breathed a word about him before, and all of a sudden there was a child in the mix. What was I supposed to do?"

"But you told me that being a stepmother was too much for you," he countered.

Beth sighed. "Being a stepmother is hard, Danny. You aren't the mom that child remembers, and yet there you are doing the hard work. It *is* a big thing to ask. Starting a family together is a whole lot different than stepping into a role with a child already there—all set up to hate you."

"He was three," Danny said, his voice low. "He wasn't going to hate you."

He'd been young, that was true. But Lana had been part of the picture, too. She was that child's real mom, and she'd be back— at least that's what Lana told her when Beth talked to her on the phone later. She'd be back. That little boy and his mom complicated everything.

Danny returned to his sweeping. Beth unbuttoned her coat and scanned the ceiling. She spotted the dangling cord attached to the attic trapdoor. It was on the far side of the store, and she headed over there while Dan cleaned.

Beth reached for the cord, but could only swipe it with her fingertips. She'd need something to stand on. She looked around and saw a stepladder. She grabbed it and planted it under the attic door. Beth put her foot on the first rung. Her balance was different these days, and this being a stepladder, she wouldn't be able to hold on to anything while she climbed. She stepped up another rung and reached up toward the cord.

"What are you doing?" Danny's voice was suddenly right next to her, and she teetered, her heart flying into her mouth. She felt the stepladder shift under her foot, and as she came down, his strong arms clamped around her. Her breath whooshed out of her lungs, and she was left gasping for breath.

She scrambled to get her feet under her again, and as she did, Danny let go of her, scowling down at her.

"Thanks," she breathed, trying to catch her breath again. Her heart still hammered in her throat. That had been close.

"I don't have the insurance to cover a pregnant woman climbing stepladders! What were you doing?"

"The attic trapdoor," she said, pointing upward feebly. "I wanted to get up there."

It seemed mildly foolhardy now, but what was she supposed to do?

"You could have *asked*!" Danny didn't seem to be calming down at all, and he reached up and pulled down the trapdoor. A ladder unfolded and landed on the tiled floor with a thunk.

"Thank you," she said with a faint smile. "Much appreciated."

"So you're climbing *that* ladder?" His tone didn't hide exactly what he thought of that idea, and that baleful glare hadn't abated, either.

"Danny, I need to get something down from there." She shook her head. "Instead of yelling at me, maybe you could give me a hand."

That was about as close to asking as he was going to get. Danny muttered something under his breath, which she should probably be grateful she hadn't heard. "What are you looking for?" he asked.

"The star for our Christmas tree…and whatever else is up there, I guess."

Danny started up the ladder, his head quickly disappearing into the attic. He was a tall man, and solid. She'd noticed how the last five years had changed him. He was tougher now, more muscled.

"So have you been this daring your whole pregnancy?" His voice was muffled.

"Yes." Up until quite recently, she'd been on her own in Edmonton. There hadn't been much choice. There was more muttering, this time a little less under his breath, and he handed down a small box.

"Is this it?"

She reached up to grab the box and opened it. "Yes, thanks. This is it."

Danny came back down the ladder. "I'll bring the rest down later. It looks like some old stashes of cups for the slushie machine, though."

Danny still looked annoyed.

"Danny, I'm sorry I left like I did. I should have stayed for more closure, I guess. I don't know what to say."

She'd ticked him off, that much was clear, and he was silent for a couple of beats.

"Be more careful, Beth," he said, then pushed the ladder back up into the attic, perhaps to keep her from getting any more ideas about climbing up there. He also scooped up the stepladder. But Beth wasn't oblivious to the dangers around here. Nor was she ungrateful for his quick catch. If she'd fallen, she could have badly hurt herself, or worse, the baby.

"Danny?"

He turned back, and for a moment he was the old Danny with those soulful eyes and the chiseled jaw.

"Thank you for catching me."

"Yeah…" He stomped back over to the corner and picked up his broom again. "No problem."

Her heart was still hammering faster than usual, and if forced, she'd admit that her near fall had scared her worse than she let on. Pregnancy wasn't easy, and it was harder still to be facing it alone. She rubbed her hand over her stomach.

She didn't have a husband to humor her or keep her from overexerting herself. She didn't have that loving, watchful spouse to care if she stretched too far or had a craving for ice cream at ten at night. And while she was a grown woman perfectly capable of caring for herself, she knew that she was more vulnerable right now. But giving in to that vulnerability wouldn't help anything. She was on her own now, and she'd be on her own after this baby was born. She'd better get used to it.

"I think I'll head back," Beth said.

"Beth, I didn't mean to bark at you." Danny scrubbed a hand through his hair.

"I know," she said. "It's okay."

"You just scared me. That's all. Sorry."

She'd scared him? His angry outburst had been covering fear for her safety?

"It's okay," she repeated. "I should probably get out of your way."

He didn't answer, which meant that her instinct was right, and he could use his space. Beth turned toward the door. When she glanced back, she found Danny's brooding gaze fixed on her. He didn't look away, and she was the one to turn and pull open the door.

"See you," he said, and she stepped outside and closed the door behind her.

The tables had turned here in North Fork. Linda was gone, and Danny was on top. Beth, as she always had been, was stuck somewhere in the middle… Not family enough for her father, not daughter enough for Linda, and not enough of whatever it would have taken for Danny to come clean and tell her his whole story. Frankly, she was tired of not being enough, and now that she had a little girl on the way, she was determined to be mom enough for one tiny person.

DAN STOOD IN his kitchen that evening making grilled cheese sandwiches. His house wasn't large, but it had a garage and a decent yard for Luke to play in. When he bought the place two years ago, it had even come with a trampoline, much to Luke's delight.

Dan could see the trampoline from the light that spilled into the backyard from his kitchen window, and it was covered in a soft layer of snow. He was hoping it would survive another year, because he couldn't afford to replace it.

He was still annoyed with Beth, and it had taken him a few hours of brooding in the store before he worked out why. It was because she sparked that protective instinct in him. She *needed* a bit of special treatment right now, whether she deserved it or not, and he couldn't provide it. And because she was pregnant, he felt obliged to do something to make things easier for her, even though what he really wanted to do was open up that can of worms with her—she'd walked out on him when he needed her most. She'd betrayed his trust, too! She'd broken his heart and left him floundering with a three-year-old who cried for his mother and to whom Dan was a stranger.

He'd needed her, and what were vows for if they didn't count in the hard times? She'd been willing to marry him, so what would have happened if Lana had come a couple of weeks later—would she have still walked out? And if not, what made a week before those vows any different? They were supposed to be saying what was in their hearts already—publicly stating an already existing commitment to each other...or so he'd thought. So yeah, she was pregnant and alone, but she'd done wrong by him five years ago, and he couldn't even address it with her. Only a complete idiot upset a pregnant woman.

A choice between a woman and his son... He knew where he'd land. Luke was his top priority, bar none. But his anger didn't take away those latent feeling he'd had for Beth, either, and left him feeling mildly guilty. It was more comfortable when things were black-and-white, when he could land easily on one side of the equation.

Dan flipped the grilled cheese and admired the golden top of the sandwich. He was always rather proud of himself when he produced a perfect grilled cheese, and glanced into the living room, where Luke was doing his home reading from school. But Luke's attention wasn't on the book. He was staring at a spot on the sofa, his brow creased.

"You okay, buddy?" Dan asked.

"Yeah." Luke tossed his book aside and ambled into the kitchen. He looked over Dan's shoulder at the grilled cheese.

"Yours is on the table," Dan said, and Luke didn't move.

"Kiera T. is adopted," Luke said. "Her birth mother visits her on her birthdays."

"Oh, yeah?" Dan eyed Luke. "You aren't adopted, you know."

"I know." Luke turned toward the table and slid into his spot. "William is adopted, too, but he doesn't know his birth mom."

It seemed like the third-grade class at the local elementary school was getting to know each other a little better. Luke had gone to school with these kids since kindergarten.

"That depends on the terms of the adoption," Dan said. "An open adoption means that it isn't a complete goodbye."

"Huh." Luke picked up his grilled cheese and took a greasy bite. "So what about *my* mom? How come I don't know her?"

There it was. Dan's stomach sank. Luke asked about his mom from time to time, but until now, he'd asked about her in the past tense, like where he was born or how he came to North Fork. Dan pulled his own grilled cheese from the pan and joined his son at the table.

"She brought you to me when she realized she couldn't take care of you," Dan said. This was the same story he always told. "And I'm really glad she did. It was the best day of my life."

That was the only version his son would ever hear, but it had taken a while for him to realize that it *was* the best day of his life, because he'd been scared, alone, heartbroken when Beth left, and unsure of how his life would work…

"Is she *allowed* to see me?" Luke asked.

The easy answer was yes, but it came with a whole lot of questions that Dan didn't know how to answer. He took a bite of his sandwich to give himself time to think.

"Well," Dan said slowly, "she can. I mean, I wouldn't keep her away. But I wouldn't let her take you back, if that's what you're worried about. I have legal custody of you, which means that your home is with me."

"Does she want to take me away?"

Shoot. He'd probably scared the kid now. Dan sighed. "No, of course not."

And a small and petty part of him hoped that Lana stayed both uninterested and very far away…at least until Luke was older.

"I don't remember her," Luke said.

"You were only three when you last saw her," Dan said. "Little kids forget."

"What's she like?" Luke fixed big brown eyes on Dan's face, waiting.

"When I knew her a long time ago, she was really pretty," Dan said. "She liked to eat her French fries with honey instead of ketchup."

"Ew," Luke said.

"Don't knock it until you've tried it, buddy," he chuckled. "It's pretty good."

"Do you talk to her sometimes?" Luke asked.

"No." She'd left contact information, and she updated that by email periodically, but that was it. She was living in Vancouver now. They didn't chat. She didn't ask about Luke. Maybe it was too painful for her—he didn't know.

"What if I wanted to meet her?" Luke asked.

Dan sighed. "It's not as simple as that."

"How come?" Luke pressed. "She's my mom. I'll bet she wants to see me."

Dan wished that were true, but if Lana had wanted to see Luke, she'd have done it long ago. And he was wary… While it was good that she'd left contact information, she had never made any overtures, and Dan had two fears: first, that she'd change her mind and try to take Luke back. Just thinking about that left him anxious. Dan couldn't afford court costs, and if she tried to just drive off with Luke… He pushed the thought back.

The second fear was that she'd show no interest at all in seeing their son, and Luke would be rejected all over again, except this time he'd be old enough to remember it.

Dan and Lana hadn't been a terribly serious couple when they'd conceived Luke. They'd met at a party and dated on and off for a bit. Dan hadn't been a mature guy at twenty-six. He'd been working hard and partying harder, and he'd been wondering if he might have a problem with alcohol, considering how much he was consuming... Lana struggled with depression, and he didn't understand it very well. Neither did she, for that matter, and they'd been fighting a lot. Then she told him she was pregnant. She said she wanted to raise the baby without him, and he was fine with her choice. He was offered a job in Alberta, and he took it.

He wasn't proud of his willingness to leave Lana with all the responsibilities now, and that was why he refused to bad-mouth Lana to Luke. If Lana had kept Luke, she might have told equally disastrous stories about him—how he'd just walked away and never looked back. He wouldn't do that to Luke...or to Lana. She was Luke's mom, and he'd speak about her with respect. Always. Even when he felt most threatened.

"Let me think it over," Dan said.

Luke was silent for a few moments,

munching his grilled cheese, then wiping his greasy fingers on the front of his shirt.

"Use a napkin," Dan said.

"Don't have one." The shirt was dirty now. It was probably high time Luke started learning how to do laundry anyway.

"Am I allowed to talk to her?" Luke asked. "Because Kiera T. can see her birth mom on Facebook, and sometimes her birth mom will comment on pictures of Kiera T. and say that she's getting really big or something."

Dan put down his sandwich. "I don't have your mom on Facebook."

"But you could search her, right?"

Luke wasn't going to give this up, Dan could tell. And he understood why it was so important to the boy, but he couldn't change facts. Evasion wasn't going to work, either. Luke was old enough to know that trick.

"*Right now*, you can't talk to her," Dan said. "I'm sorry. It's my job to decide what's best for you, and tracking down your mom wouldn't be a good idea. *Right now.* When you're older it might be different."

Luke turned his attention back to his meal. Dan had known this day would come, but somehow, he'd thought he'd be more prepared for it.

Lana could be unpredictable, and that freaked him out. When he'd told Beth about his son and his ex-girlfriend's demand that he take over with him, Beth had asked to talk to Lana after she'd dropped off Luke. That had seemed very levelheaded of Beth, and perhaps he should have seen what was coming then, but he'd been optimistic. So he'd given Beth Lana's phone number, and it was only later—when Beth dumped him—that she told him that Lana had promised to be in the middle of their life from that moment on. She wanted her due.

Lana had managed to intimidate Beth rather effectively. But he couldn't blame Lana, because in some ways she'd been right—the full weight of raising their child shouldn't have been on her shoulders. Dan had a responsibility, too—both financially and emotionally. Except Beth hadn't known about that when she agreed to marry him, and when she'd weighed it out in her heart, she decided that the headache Lana promised to be wasn't worth it.

Lana had never come through on that

threat. She'd talked Beth into a corner, and perhaps enjoyed it. Then she'd gone away. Lana wasn't predictable in the least.

And neither was Beth… He'd honestly believed that they'd get through it all together. He couldn't have been more wrong. And while Lana had disappeared to Vancouver, Beth had returned. He hadn't seen that one coming, either.

Seeing Beth again had reminded Dan about how detrimental her stepmother's rejection had been, and he wouldn't allow Luke to go through the same thing again with his own mother. The world was a hard place, and Luke was too young to face the ugliness.

CHAPTER FOUR

BETH RUBBED A hand over her belly, feeling that strange, rolling motion of the baby moving inside her. She still wasn't used to this, but she never got tired of feeling those wriggles. Riley didn't have much more room in there, and Beth felt every stretch and jab. She tucked her hair behind her ears and looked down at the ripples of the baby's foot moving across the top of her stomach.

"Hi, you…" Beth said softly. She stood in the kitchen, a mug of herbal tea steaming in front of her on the counter. She was thinking that she'd much rather have a doughnut right about now. Or cake. Chocolate cake. Black forest cake—that was it! The closest she could find to her craving in the cupboards were some crackers and hazelnut spread. It would have to do.

These winter mornings were cold, and the house wasn't as well insulated as it could have been, so a draft wafted through the room and curled around her legs. Outside a bluebird was at the bird feeder hanging from a tree branch, and a squirrel hung back, seeming to sense it was outgunned by the bigger, meaner bird. It would do well to back off, Beth thought ruefully.

Her cell phone buzzed, and she looked down to see a text from her friend Abby.

Are you busy? Feel up to some company?

Beth smiled and typed back: Not busy. Where are you?

In front of your house.

Beth chuckled and headed through the living room, where Granny sat watching TV. Beth pulled open the front door and poked her head out. A red hatchback was parked in their drive, and Abby got out with a wave.

Abayomi, or Abby as everyone called her, was short and plump with dark skin that glowed with health and hair done in a sleek bob. She was of Nigerian descent—both of her parents were doctors who settled in

North Fork when she was a young girl. North Fork, being quite far north in Alberta, suffered from a lack of medical professionals, and when Abby's family arrived, the entire town was filled with relief to have two full-time doctors setting up right here in town. Abby's mother was an ob-gyn, and her father had been a surgeon in Nigeria but established himself as a family doctor in Canada.

"Oh. My. Goodness!" Abby's hand flew to her face, and she slammed her door and headed toward the front steps. "Look at you, girl! I knew about the pregnancy, but I had to see this for myself."

"In all my glory." Beth rolled her eyes. "Hurry up and get in here. It's cold."

Abby picked up her pace, and after hugs and the removal of boots and her coat, Abby stood back to look at Beth.

"You're ready to pop!" Abby exclaimed, putting a hand on Beth's belly. "So how come you didn't call me when you got back?"

"It's…" Beth shot her friend an apologetic look. "I'm overwhelmed. There's a lot on my plate right now, and—"

And Abby was happily married. After Abby's wedding, their friendship had grown more distanced because Abby was busy with her husband and Beth was, frankly, a little jealous. Abby's happiness reminded her of the wedding she'd walked away from, so it was easier to focus on friends who didn't know her history.

Abby squeezed Beth's hand. "Forgiven. Just don't repeat it. I'm here for you."

"Abayomi," Granny said, pushing herself up from her recliner. "Aren't you a sight for sore eyes. Come over here and give me a hug."

Abby gave Granny a hug, and after some pleasantries, Granny resettled in front of the TV, and Beth and Abby went into the kitchen to chat.

"So how are you?" Beth asked. "How is married life treating you?"

"The honeymoon is over and we drive each other nuts," Abby said with a short laugh. "But Clint is worth it."

"How long did you date, again?" Beth asked. It had been fast, and there hadn't been a wedding for anyone to attend. Beth had bought her friend a present online and had it shipped. That had been four years ago now, near enough to her own canceled wedding to sting.

"Oh, we were crazy. We dated for six months, then he popped the question and we eloped." Abby glanced around. "So does this mean that you and Collin are back together, or…"

"No, still very much broken up," Beth said with a tight smile.

"And he left you pregnant." Abby shook her head in disgust. "I hope you're going for a pound of flesh over that. You know that Clint's a lawyer—"

"No, no. I wasn't pregnant when we broke up." Beth licked her lips. "This was…a different mistake."

"Oh." Abby paused. "Okay…"

"For once, Abby, I did something spontaneous." She shot her friend a pleading look. She didn't need judgment right now. She needed a little sympathy. "The father is some guy from a bar. It only took four drinks and being dumped…and it was the stupidest thing I've ever done."

"No, I get it," Abby replied. "I always thought Collin was a bit dry. I only saw him those few times, but I didn't think he was a

great match for you. Not a bad guy, just…
unimpressive, I guess."

Beth smiled ruefully. "I think I settled in
a lot of ways with Collin. He was good on
paper, you know? He was—ironically, he
was the kind of guy Linda approved of! But
after Danny, I was tired of risk. I just wanted
someone stable and safe." She sighed.

Danny had made her feel things she'd
never felt since. No guy could match the
way he made her heart pound. He'd been
romantic and sweet…but it was more than
romantic gestures. It was the way her heart
lurched when he looked into her eyes or the
butterflies she felt when he held her hand.
She'd loved him, but when she found out how
much he'd hidden, her confidence had been
severely shaken. How could she trust him
with the rest of her life if he couldn't trust
her with his personal history?

Besides, she'd seen the way Danny had
fallen in love with his boy. As he should—
it was only right. But she didn't share his
tenderness—she'd still been in shock! And
she'd suddenly seen herself in a role she'd
never imagined before: stepmother. She'd

be in Linda's position, taking a back seat to his child…

"Have you seen Danny yet?" Abby asked.

"Yeah, he bought my dad's store," she said. "So I've been going over there to get some of the things we want to keep for memories."

"And what did he think about your pregnancy?" Abby asked with a grin. "Because you are adorable. You have to know that. You're all out front."

"He yelled at me when I tried to climb a stepladder." Beth chuckled. Was it wrong to feel a bit satisfied at having gotten a rise out of him? Even if it hadn't been intentional, and if he'd ended up being right.

"Danny hollered at you?" Abby laughed. "He's normally so…stoic."

"Apparently, I can still annoy him like no one else," Beth replied drily. "I've still got that, at least."

"He's single right now," Abby added. "He has Luke, you're expecting your baby…"

"Abby, he lied to me." Beth shook her head. "Having a kid is heart-level stuff. He should have told me. If he could hold back his son, what else did he hold back?"

"I know." Abby sighed. "He was wrong."

"He was more than wrong," Beth said. "He wasn't the man I thought he was."

Abby nodded. "I get it. I don't know what I'd have done in the same situation." She paused. "So, what's the plan here? Are you back for good?"

"I think so," Beth replied. "I'll have to find a job, and I'll raise my daughter. I don't have a lot of choice right now."

A baby changed absolutely everything. Life wasn't going to be easy, and the reality of her situation had been growing heavier over the last few days.

"Abby, I'm scared." Beth blinked back tears. "This wasn't the plan."

"What you need is to get busy!" Abby said.

"You are the first person to say that," Beth sighed. "Everyone else tells me to put my feet up."

"Oh, forget them. I know *you*." Abby leaned forward. "Get involved with something. You know what I'm doing right now? I'm volunteering with the North Fork Christmas pageant. We were in it every year when we were kids, remember?"

"I loved it," Beth said with a smile.

"Well, it takes a lot of people to run. We could use more volunteers."

"Yeah?" Beth paused, thinking. "I can't bend or lift very much. I'm not sure how useful I'd be…"

"We'll give you something to do that involves sitting or standing." Abby glanced down at Beth's belly. "Or just sitting. Whatever you want. Just come. It'll be fun, and you'll see other people and get out of your head a little bit. It's Christmas, after all!"

Abby cocked her head, waiting, eyebrows raised.

"Is it at town hall this year?" Beth asked.

"It's at town hall *every* year," Abby said with a roll of her eyes. "Nothing changes in North Fork. You know that."

"Okay, well…sure. You're right. I should get out more."

Abby grinned in satisfaction. "Perfect. Come for the practice tomorrow at six. They'll put you to work. That's a promise."

Beth needed to get out of the house, away from the store that only reminded her of how hard her family had landed. And she needed to wipe her heart free from both Collin and

Danny. Neither of them had been good for her, and she knew it.

Besides, Beth had plans to make. She was going to be a mother, and everything would be different. She might not have the right man by her side in this, but she also didn't have the wrong one. She'd raise her daughter well, and that took some forethought. Danny was in the past, and she certainly wasn't going to get distracted now.

DAN SLOWED HIS truck to a crawl. Granny was walking down the sidewalk, her red coat pulled close around her and her chin held high. She marched with determination, not even giving his rumbling motor a glance.

It was cold out there today—as it was every day this time of year. This was northern Canada, after all, and the citizens of North Fork didn't let the weather stop them from anything. He'd moved here from Vancouver, and the mild weather he'd experienced in that coastal city hadn't prepared him for the driving cold. Yet over the past almost nine years that he'd spent in Alberta, he'd found himself joining the other locals in their perverse pleasure in treating the coldest days like spring.

Dan pushed the button to lower the passenger-side window, and he slowed down enough to keep pace with her.

"Granny!" he called.

The old woman looked over at him, an arch expression on her face. When she saw Dan, she smiled and paused her steps.

"Oh, hello, Daniel," she said sweetly. "How are you doing?"

"I'm good," he said. There was something about Granny Thomas that brought out his manners. "How are you doing?"

"Just fine, thank you, Daniel. Have a good day," she said, gave him a cordial nod and started walking again.

Dan heaved a sigh. She could be difficult when she was on some personal mission.

"Granny," he called again. "Where are you going?"

"I'm going—" She stopped, frowned, shook her head. "I don't remember. It'll come back to me."

"Why don't I give you a ride?" Danny asked. "It's cold out."

"It's not cold," she said with a bat of her

hand. "It's winter." As if the two things were separate experiences.

"But Beth said she needed you for something," he countered.

"Oh…" Granny sighed. "Wedding plans, no doubt. You should be lending her more of a hand, young man."

She came to the door, and Dan leaned over and pulled the handle to let her in. Granny was spryer than most people knew, and she hopped up into the cab without difficulty.

"Ralph didn't do much for our wedding," Granny said as she buckled up. "But those times were different. Men were expected to show up dressed in a suit. That was it. But these days, men are much more involved, Daniel."

She wasn't going to let this drop, he could tell. Dan gave her a pained smile. He'd been pretty involved in planning their wedding five years ago. At least he'd thought he'd been. Maybe he was wrong about that.

"And speaking of how times have changed," Granny went on, "men are in the delivery room now."

She gave him another meaningful look, and Dan wished he could disappear into his seat. Fetching Granny had been a lot easier before Beth came back, when Granny would sit quietly in the passenger seat and murmur about how Ralph just hated it when she was late.

"Have you considered moving the wedding date up?" Granny asked when Dan hadn't answered. "I know this is delicate, dear, but I think it would mean a lot to Beth."

If only Granny remembered that Beth had been the one to dump *him*. This wasn't just about him and Beth anymore—Luke was in the mix now. Dan signaled a turn onto the Thomases' street.

"We should probably talk about that," he said diplomatically. It seemed easier to play along than to explain things and upset her. She wasn't *his* grandmother. "Don't worry, Granny. Everything will be okay."

Funny—that's what he used to tell Luke when he'd cry for his mother. "Don't worry, Luke. Everything will be okay." And Luke would cry himself out in his father's arms. Because Dan couldn't promise that Lana would come back…ever. All he could promise was that one day it'd be all right. Or close to all right. Sometimes, that just had to do.

Dan pulled into the Thomases' driveway and got out first to give Granny a hand down. Then he accompanied her to the door. The early-afternoon sunlight sparkled on the snow. Granny opened the front door and went straight in.

Beth stood in the living room, a slightly frantic expression on her face. She wore leggings and a knit turtleneck sweater that was an icy-blue color, bringing out the blue of her eyes as her gaze whipped between Dan and her grandmother. He wasn't supposed to be staring at her, but he was. She was gorgeous, and an eight-month pregnant belly didn't change that.

"Granny!" Beth gasped. "I was looking for you. Where were you?"

"I was just—" Granny frowned, shook her head. "I don't know. I was out, I think. Oh, hello, Daniel." The old woman turned and smiled at Dan. "That's right. We were talking about the wedding, weren't we? Why don't I leave you two to discuss. I could close my eyes for a few minutes."

Granny bent to take off her boots. It took a few minutes for her to get out of all her winter wear, and as she quietly worked at it, Dan and Beth exchanged a look. Granny was getting worse—Dan could tell. She was more confused, and this time she'd wandered farther than the store. But his focus right now was on Beth and those fluid blue eyes and the way she cradled her belly with one porcelain hand... Why did she have to be so beautiful? Why couldn't she have lost some of that sparkle over the last few years? It would have made her return easier for him, made her a little easier to file into the past.

Granny finished hanging her coat and headed for the recliner.

"Could I talk to you?" Dan said, nodding toward the kitchen.

"Yeah, sure." Beth looked at her grandmother for a moment, then sighed and led the way into the kitchen.

"I had no idea she'd even left!" Beth ran a hand through her hair. "Abby dropped by and Granny was in the living room. We visited for a while, Abby left, and Granny was gone."

"Granny strikes me as the stealthy sort," Dan agreed.

"Where was she?" Beth asked.

"On Butternut Street."

"That far?" Beth heaved a sigh. "We're going to need to put an alarm on the doors or something."

"But that's not all…" Dan wasn't sure how to say this delicately, so he figured he'd just plow right ahead. "She's stuck on this idea that you and I are getting married."

Color rose in Beth's cheeks. "I'm sorry about that." She shrugged faintly. "She's been doing that ever since I got back. I must have sparked something."

"Have you tried telling her the truth?" he asked.

"I did—when I first got back," Beth said. "She was frantic, worried about me, obsessed with all the details involved with canceling a wedding… It only made things worse."

"I was afraid of that," he admitted. "So what are we supposed to do?"

"Play along?" She met his eyes uncertainly. "I know it's a lot to ask. It's the same idea as telling her that Grandpa has gone out for milk. It just seems to comfort her. It lets her stay in a happy place."

"And our wedding made her happy," he concluded.

"I never realized how invested she'd

been," Beth said. She smoothed a hand over her stomach, and he followed the movement with his gaze. "I mean, until her dementia got worse. With her mind going into the past like this, we're getting to see how she felt about things…about people."

"About me?" Dan said, smiling wanly.

"I suppose." Beth laughed softly. "So what do you think? Are you willing to play along when Granny's with us?"

Dan sighed. He didn't want to, but he doubted Beth wanted this, either. It was reliving a painful time in his own life to comfort Granny during this confusing time in hers. But Beth was right. If they simply told her the truth, it would only upset her. It would be cruel to do that repeatedly.

"I could try," he agreed.

"So could I." Beth sighed. "I do appreciate it. I know it's a lot to ask."

Dan shook his head. "It's a weird situation."

Beth turned away from him and opened a cupboard. She stretched to reach something, but her belly wouldn't let her close enough.

"What are you trying to get?" he asked.

"Hazelnut spread," she said, giving up.

"I'm craving black forest cake like you wouldn't believe."

Dan shot her a quizzical look, and she shrugged. "Trust me, it connects."

Dan passed her the hazelnut spread and could see her visibly relax at the sight of it.

"Pregnancy craving?" he asked.

"Cookies and cakes and carbs," she said, unscrewing the cap. "Those seem to be my cravings, and this morning I realized that the one thing to complete me heart and soul would be black forest cake. Since I don't have that, I'm making do. You want some?"

He shook his head. He didn't know about this stage of things—he'd been long gone by the time Lana had been showing, and seeing Beth now brought back all those regrets. Beth smeared some spread onto a cracker and popped it into her mouth.

"So…" He cleared his throat. "Do you need me to do a bakery run or something? How urgent is this?"

Beth smiled. "I'm good. No worries. A few carrot sticks wouldn't kill me, either."

She dipped a spoon into the hazelnut spread and brought it up domed in chocolate goo. She began nibbling around the side of the spoon. So much for carrot sticks—not that he blamed her.

"How have things been around here?" Dan asked.

"With my dad, you mean?" she asked.

"Yeah." Was it wrong of him to care? He'd been willing to join their family five years ago, and that had to count for something.

"Dad is kind of depressed," Beth said. "As you'd expect."

"Is he writing?" he asked. Rick had always been plugging away on something. His books took a couple of years to finish, but that didn't mean he wasn't constantly working.

"No." She sighed. "I haven't seen him write a word since I got back. Instead of facing everything at once, he's tackling the problems he thinks he can fix. Like child support."

"The father isn't paying?" Dan frowned. "What kind of guy were you with, Beth?"

He still felt protective of her, whether he had the right to or not. At the very least, he'd expected that Beth's guy would be head and shoulders above the likes of him, but if he wasn't even supporting his child... At least Dan had done the right thing eventually. Maybe this guy would, too.

Beth sipped some chocolate hazelnut off the spoon, then licked her lips. "What kind of guy? The wrong one."

"It isn't that complicated to get child support," Dan said. "I could show you the government websites that get the process started—"

"No." Her tone was decided, and he stopped. "Does Lana pay you support?"

"No." He cleared his throat. "I'm fine. I can take care of Luke on my own. Besides, Lana is in a rough spot—has been for years." He paused. Her expression had changed. "What?"

"You told me about Lana," she said. "You'd always said that you two weren't that serious."

"And we weren't."

"But a child together?" She raised her eyebrows. "I don't care if that pregnancy was planned or not, that makes things a whole lot more serious."

Dan sighed. "You have a point, but emotionally—"

"Emotionally?" Her eyes snapped fire.

"That's semantics, Danny! I told you everything about my past, my hang-ups, my feelings, my hopes for the future. I was an open book with you. But you—" she looked around as if searching for the word "—weren't."

"The last I had seen Lana, she'd told me she had taken a pregnancy test, and she was done with me," he said. "She never even told me when he was born. She told me about six months later, and she reiterated that she didn't want me in the picture. It didn't exactly feel real." It was a stupid thing to say to a pregnant woman, and he knew it. "I was wrong, okay?"

"Yes, you were." She nodded. "But you know what hurts the most? You didn't trust me enough to tell me. You were a dad. There was a little person out there with your DNA. You had to feel *something*."

"Of course I felt something!" Dan erupted. "And a whole lot of what I felt was shame!"

Beth didn't answer, but the fire in her eyes dwindled, and she dropped her gaze.

"I walked away from my child, Beth." His voice wavered. "I hated myself for that. Forgive me for not wanting you to hate me, too."

They stared at each other for a couple

of beats. These were old hurts, ones he'd thought he'd dealt with, but standing here with Beth, it all felt raw. She'd wanted him to share his feelings—but she came from a rather privileged position. She came from a well-respected family who struggled with their own issues, granted, but would she have understood what his life had been like in Vancouver? How empty he felt? How stupid he felt for getting involved with a woman he knew he had no future with?

Beth sighed. "And now Lana's the one who walked out. And you're on your own."

Yes, Lana had dropped Luke off and disappeared, and he'd felt angry about that, too, but he'd made his peace with it. Maybe it was even for the best.

"She struggles with depression," he said. "And she's been self-medicating with street drugs. It's only gotten worse. She couldn't send money if she wanted to."

Beth put down the spoon she'd been holding in one hand, forgotten.

"So why aren't *you* going for support payments?" he said. "Are you scared that the dad will want to share custody or something?"

Beth shook her head. "You know how you

don't want to talk about some stuff?" she asked with a bitter smile.

"I'll talk," Dan said. It had been five years, and he wasn't trying to marry her—this was different now. "Because I'd understand it if you were scared that the dad would want his rights. I live every day with the fear that Lana will decide she wants to be in Luke's life again. I've been doing my best to raise him and love him, and the thought of her just waltzing back in and taking him for half the week…or taking off with him—" His chest clenched at the very thought. He cleared his throat. "I understand, is all."

"It isn't that." She raised her blue gaze to meet his.

"Then what is it?"

"I don't know who the father is."

Dan hadn't expected to hear that. He frowned, looked away as he processed that information.

"And no, I wasn't sleeping around," she added. "I was monogamous to a fault until Collin dumped me for a job on the East Coast. My girlfriend convinced me I needed to let loose for an evening and wash the memory of Collin out of my system with a

steady flow of alcohol. Long story short—"
She gestured to her belly.

"So you really don't know who…"

"No idea," she replied. "Except for an
Australian accent."

"Okay, so child support is out," he agreed.
That was obvious. She was very much on
her own.

"And for some reason, telling my dad
that—it's harder than I thought. I don't want
to disappoint him."

"Hey, that's how babies are made." He shot
her a wry smile. "Biology."

"It's just the timing. This wasn't planned…
I'm not ready, and I'm a grown woman. I'm
not supposed to be coming back to my father
for help. We're past that. We're *supposed* to
be past that."

Dan shrugged. "But with this baby, everything is going to change," he said. "You're a
mom now, and it changes all those roles, including how you relate to your father."

"Tell my dad that." She shook her head.
"He doesn't see it yet."

"Then it's your job to point it out."

There was no other way around it. But
relationships *would* change, and so would

Beth. She wouldn't have the luxury of pleasing everyone anymore.

Beth sighed. "I'm sure you're right."

Dan glanced at his watch, more to break the awkward moment than anything else. He'd said more than he'd planned today, and he felt a nervous tension rising inside him. He needed to get out, to get away, get his head on straight.

"I'd better go," he said. "Luke will be off school soon, and I have some things to finish up."

"Okay." She gave a quick nod. "Well… Thanks for bringing Granny home."

"No problem." He met her gaze for a moment, and it all felt so familiar that it ached. Yet everything was different now. For her, for him… They were now two single parents trying to figure things out alone.

"What I told you…about the father—" she began.

"My lips are sealed," he interjected. "That's not my secret to tell."

She'd trusted him with some sensitive information, and he felt the responsibility there.

"Thank you." She visibly relaxed. "I really appreciate it, Danny."

They might not be engaged anymore, but they were both parents now. She could count on some solidarity. He of all people could appreciate how complicated parenting could get.

CHAPTER FIVE

ABBY WAS TRUE to her word, and when Beth arrived at the town hall the next evening for the rehearsal, everyone was expecting her. Beth knew a fair number of the volunteers, and if she didn't know them personally, they had connections in common. A school friend's older sister was working the lights; the drugstore owner's brother-in-law was directing the band. North Fork was small enough that no one was a complete stranger.

Town hall was a large brick building on Main Street, next door to the bank. That town hall had been standing for over ninety years, ever since North Fork had been founded. Local government meetings were held here, as well as all the mayor and aldermen's election speeches. In the summer, the Food of the World Fair was also hosted in town hall. Around North Fork, the exotic foods available were mostly Ukrainian and Polish, so there were a lot of variations on the cabbage roll and the pierogi. When Abby's family moved into the area, there was great excitement at the prospect of new culinary offerings. The mayor himself visited the Oduwales and begged them to be a part of the food fair the following summer. It was the most popular fair they'd ever had, and it was also how Beth met Abby. Their booths were side by side—pierogies next to Nigerian dodo and akara, which were deep-fried delicacies. They'd both sold out in record time, and the girls became fast friends in the process.

But winter brought the Christmas pageant, and everyone was included. Abby's family was invited to take part that year, too, as North Fork did what North Fork did best— gave every last person a job to do. It turned out that Abby could both act and sing. She had no hope of escaping the pageant again, and she'd played a lead part every year since.

"Are you in the pageant this year?" Beth asked her friend.

"I'm Angel Number Four," Abby replied.

"I thought this was *A Christmas Carol*?"

"It's *A Christmas Carol* with some

tweaks." Abby winked. "We found some gorgeous angel costumes and didn't want to wait to use them."

Beth laughed. "Whatever works."

As Beth and Abby walked inside, they were met with a barrage of busy people. Beth gave hugs to the people she knew, tolerated the belly touches and allowed Abby to lead her over to a section backstage where kids were being fitted for their costumes.

"Beth!" called an excited voice. Beth looked over to see Mrs. Connolly, a local seamstress. She had a pincushion on her wrist and a child standing on a milk crate in front of her.

"When are you due?" Mrs. Connolly asked with a smile.

"January fourth."

"That's so exciting! So...the dad?"

Beth and Abby exchanged a look, and Abby grimaced.

"Out of the picture," Beth said.

"Say no more." Mrs. Connolly tugged at the dress of the little girl in front of her. Thank goodness for small ears—it effectively stopped any more awkward conversation.

"Beth is here to help out, and Marg suggested you could use a hand in costumes," Abby said. "Can you put her to work?"

"Without a doubt," Mrs. Connolly replied past a pin held between her lips. A small boy stood to the side, waiting with a rumpled gray wig in his hands. "I haven't seen Linda in a long time. How is she?"

"She moved back to Edmonton," Beth replied.

"Well, that's understandable, considering. I don't expect you'll see her much," the older woman said. "I should have gotten her email address or something. I miss having tea with her. You don't happen to have it, do you?"

"No, sorry." Beth cleared her throat. Linda had had friends and work associates at the elementary school where she was a secretary, but if she wanted to keep in touch with them, that was up to her. Beth wasn't going to run messages for her ex-stepmother.

"Oh!" Mrs. Connolly turned toward the boy who was waiting. "Luke here has been having trouble with his wig—it's a tad too big, so we'll have to figure something out for him. He, um… Well, you must have met him when he was rather small." She paused, glanced over at Beth with a tense look on her face and cleared her throat uncomfortably.

Luke? Beth's heart skipped a beat. This was Danny's son?

"Go on over to Beth," Mrs. Connolly said, a little too brightly, then she turned to Beth. "Is this…okay?"

"I'm fine." Beth forced a smile to her face. "It was a long time ago."

Mrs. Connolly nodded. "My box of tricks is right behind you. Get creative."

"Have fun," Abby said, shooting Beth a cautious look. "I've got to get back to rehearsal. You'll be okay?"

"Of course," Beth said, and she looked past her friend toward the little boy who approached with a gray-haired wig in hand. He didn't look much like the three-year-old she'd seen at Danny's place when he'd called her over saying, "This is big, babe. I'll explain when you get here…" She'd been shocked when she saw the toddler, angry when she'd realized how much her fiancé had hidden, and then terrified, because she'd seen the way Danny looked at the boy…

I'll figure something out, Danny had said. *He's…mine. It'll take some adjustment, but*

I can do this. He's my son, and it's time, I guess. My God, Beth...he's mine.

That sleeping toddler might have been his, but Beth had never felt more distanced from Danny. He'd looked down at his son, and she'd seen he was filled with emotion about what that meant for him. It was understandable, of course, but she hadn't known where she fit. It had taken several hours before Danny had used the word *we* to mean him and Beth. Until then it had meant him and this sleeping boy. He was a father, but what was she?

This child in front of her wasn't a toddler anymore. Luke was wearing black pants that were a tad too loose, a dress shirt and what looked like a man's tie. He had Danny's dark hair and eyes.

"Hi," Beth said, trying to sound normal. "I'm supposed to help you with that wig."

"Okay." Luke came closer and handed it over. "It keeps falling over my eyes."

She took the wig from his hands, darting an extra look at the boy. He looked like his father—there was no denying that. Beth glanced over at Mrs. Connolly, but she was busy with another child, leaving Beth and

Luke in relative privacy. When Beth turned back to Luke, he shot her a brilliant smile, and she was surprised into returning it.

"Are you gonna fix it?" he asked.

"I'll try. What part are you playing?" Beth asked.

"I'm a townsperson," he replied. "An elderly townsperson. And I sing two lines."

"Do you?" She grabbed a milk crate and moved it up in front of her. "Have a seat. We'll see if we can keep your wig on, old man."

Luke grinned again, but this time impishly. "You aren't supposed to call old people old."

"They aren't tricked when you call them elderly, either," she quipped.

"I thought elderly was younger than old," Luke said.

"No, sorry." She examined the wig and then looked at the box of pins, needles, scraps and thread. "But that's okay. There comes a point when no one can deny it."

"Are you—" He stopped.

"Am I old?" she asked and laughed.

"No, are you going to have a baby?"

"I suppose there is no denying that, either.

Yes, I am." She held out the wig. "Put this on, and we'll see where it's loose."

Luke put it on, and she tugged here and there, seeing where a little tightening might help keep the wig in one place. Riley squirmed as Beth leaned forward, crowding the baby's space.

"I saw something move!" Luke exclaimed.

"Yes, she just kicked. I felt that, too." She plucked the wig off Luke's head. "She's pretty active in there right now."

"It's a baby girl?" he asked.

"Sure is."

"What's her name?"

His question was so innocent and wide-eyed that while Beth didn't like to share the name too early—when people might weigh in with their opinions—she didn't see the harm in telling this curious kid.

"Her name is Riley," Beth said. It felt nice to say it aloud.

"There's a girl in my class named Riley," Luke said. "She's okay, as far as girls go. She has long hair."

That was likely a high compliment at this age, and Beth smiled as she threaded a needle.

"So what are your two lines?" she asked.

"I sing about how the weather is cold and the young men are bold and the blessings are twofold," he said.

"That's a mouthful," she said.

"I sing it with Tracy Porter. Well, I sing my two lines by myself, but Tracy is singing the rest of the song, so…"

"Is she related to Lisa Porter?" Beth asked. Lisa had always been musical, and she'd even put out a CD a couple of years ago. She was as close to a professional musician as North Fork had.

"I think that's her mom," Luke said. "Anyway, Tracy knows how to sing."

"I'm sure you can sing, too," Beth said.

"I dunno."

"They gave you two lines, Luke," Beth said. "They don't give two lines to just anyone."

"They kind of do," Luke replied with a grimace, and Beth smothered a smile. "My dad says to just imagine everyone in their underwear, but I think that would just make me feel embarrassed, because if someone's in their underwear, a bully probably pulled down their pants. And that's just not nice."

"Hmm." Beth nodded slowly. "That's a

good point, Luke. Your dad was in this pageant one year. So he knows what he's talking about, though."

Beth had talked him into doing a small adult role. He never did fully forgive her for that.

"He never told me that!" Luke fixed her with a look of interest. "What part did he get?"

"I think he was Shepherd Number Five, or something like that." She lowered her voice conspiratorially. "He didn't get a line."

"No line?" Luke frowned. "Like nothing?"

"Nothing." Beth gave him a significant look. "Just goes to show you that not everyone gets *two* lines."

"Were you in this pageant?" Luke asked.

"Oh, yeah. Every year when I was a kid."

"Did you get lines?"

"Sometimes," she admitted. "Well, most of the time. I was a good memorizer."

The only reason Danny had taken the part that year was because they needed a responsible adult with a motorcycle license to drive a motorcycle across the stage. Their pageants didn't lean toward the traditional. Danny had taken the part as a favor to Beth, who was helping direct that year. She'd never seen the rugged Danny look more out of his element than on the stage. A little like someone who'd been pantsed by a bully.

"I'm a good memorizer, too," Luke said, then he paused as if putting it all together in his head. "Were you my dad's friend?"

There it was—the question she should have sidestepped. She hadn't been able to be this boy's stepmother, but she didn't want him to know that. That would be like a personal rejection of the kid.

"I was his friend." That was the simplest way of putting it, at least. "We were very good friends. In fact, you look a lot like him."

"I know." Obviously, Luke had heard that a lot, and it was strange to look at this pint-size version of Danny Brockwood. This was the child she'd been so afraid of five years ago, and while he seemed much less intimidating now, she still knew that she'd made the right choice. Wig fitting and stepmothering were two very different roles, and she'd seen the way Danny looked at his son that night. Danny had stared at his sleeping boy with a look of awe and heartbreaking love.

She'd seen it clear as day—if she married Danny, she'd be stepping into Linda's role as outsider in the family. She'd never be this child's real mom, but Danny *would* be his real dad...

"What's your name?" Luke asked.

"Beth."

"I'm Luke." He held out his hand to shake, and she took his small hand in hers. She already knew his name, but he seemed to like the formal introduction.

"It's a pleasure, old man."

"All mine, old lady," he quipped, and Beth laughed, then turned back to her stitching. Luke was sweet and likable, and she found her earlier anxiety at the very thought of him start to evaporate. He was just a kid...and it had been five years since she'd called off the wedding. Maybe that was enough time for all of them to move on.

She finished the inside of the wig and tried it on Luke's head once more. It wasn't a perfect fit, but it was significantly better. "What do you think?"

"It won't go in my eyes now," Luke said. "Thanks."

"You're very welcome," she said. "Go make us proud."

Luke started off, adjusting the wig as he went, then he turned back.

"Not even one line?" he asked.

"Not one. He drove a motorcycle, though," she said. "Ask him about that!"

Luke grinned. "Okay, 'bye."

As Luke disappeared into the milling actors and volunteers, Beth watched him go with a strange feeling in her heart. He was a sweet boy, and Danny was obviously doing a good job raising him. Would it have been so bad to be Luke Brockwood's stepmom?

But a sweet kid didn't change facts, and parenting was far more complicated than anyone could see on the outside. Everyone in town thought that Linda was a great stepmom. She might not have been overly affectionate, but she'd kept two teens in line, kept them well dressed and polite. Beth and Michael had gone with Rick and Linda to church, and they'd probably looked like a successfully blended family. Except they weren't.

And seeing Danny's son reminded Beth of Linda and her constant attempts to inject herself into Rick's relationship with his daughter. Linda was jealous of their connection, and in this moment, watching Luke disappear into a crowd of kids, she could understand a little of what Linda must have felt in raising a heartbroken girl who needed love but didn't want it from her. Being a stepparent meant doing all the work of raising a child but not having the same kind of connection that everyone else shared. That would be hard, Beth thought—at least it seemed that way to her. She'd had a couple of friends with stepfathers growing up, but she'd been the only one with a stepmom.

"My sleeve is torn," a small voice said, and Beth looked up to see a little girl in what was probably a townsperson dress. Beth smiled and beckoned her over.

"Let's see what we can do."

DAN PARKED HIS truck along Main Street and turned off the engine. Luke's rehearsal would be over soon. He was proud of his son. Luke was getting more independent, and he had taken some real pride in his part in the pageant. He'd been singing his lines over and over again.

Two whole lines. Dan might be prouder than Luke was, truth be told, and he couldn't wait to sit in the folding chairs and hear Luke's two lines. This was a big deal for a dad.

Dan smiled to himself and hopped out of the truck. The first Christmas that Luke spent in North Fork, he'd been the biggest baby Jesus ever at the age of three. In the years that followed, he'd been cast as Joyful Child Number Six or something like that— just a kid on the stage pretending to play in the snow, sweating in his snowsuit. And this year he got his very first solo lines. He'd been practicing for weeks, and Dan probably knew them better than he did at this point.

Dan had never been terribly interested in the pageant before he'd gotten custody of his son, but having Luke in his home had changed things. He watched other families more closely, trying to figure out what they were doing right. How else was he supposed to figure out child-rearing? And one thing he remembered from Beth's family was that they always participated in that pageant.

Luke hadn't been first choice for baby Jesus, but when the Nelson baby had come down with croup, they'd needed someone to fill in, and at that time there were no other babies—at least no other babies with mothers willing to have them carried around by a thirteen-year-old Mary onstage. So Luke, in a blue pull-up diaper and wrapped in a white bedsheet, had been cast. Mary had staggered under the weight of him.

Dan got out of his truck and headed down the street, shrugging his coat higher up his neck. The nights were getting colder now that December was here, and his cheeks stung from the biting breeze. The sun had slipped below the horizon, leaving the velvet darkness, softened by streetlights and a full moon.

He was more shaken than he liked to admit by Beth's return to North Fork. He'd just found his groove—or at least that's how it felt. He had a solid business plan, a new retail space, and he was finally becoming the man he'd wanted to be all these years—a business owner, a success. Except Luke was starting to struggle with his mother's abandonment, and Dan didn't need any distractions. Which meant Beth's return was terribly timed. He needed peace and quiet—

not the emotional upheaval that naturally came along with Beth Thomas.

Dan trotted up the front steps of town hall. The sound of voices and discordant music filtered out into the night. He pulled open the door and stepped into a wall of warmth and noise. He followed the sound of the piano toward the auditorium, stepping aside as a group of little girls in angel outfits came tripping out and beelined for the ladies' room in a flurry of giggles and chatter.

He stopped in the auditorium and looked around, searching for Luke. It took him a couple of minutes, but then he spotted him on the far side of the room, his arms held out at his sides as if he was being measured. Maybe they were adding to the costumes.

"Hi, Abby," Dan said, and the shorter woman smiled in return as she passed. She was dressed in an angel costume, too, the white material making her dark skin glow in contrast.

"I've got to check on the girls," she said. "Sorry to run."

"Yeah, yeah—"

Abby hurried past, and Dan headed over to his son. Luke dropped his arms and shifted to the side, exposing the person doing the measuring, and Dan's heart skipped a beat. She saw him at the same moment, and color bloomed in her cheeks. She was seated on a chair, a measuring tape in hand, and she raised one hand in a wave. Luke turned then, and when Dan came up, his son said, "Hi, Dad."

"Hi," Dan said, and he put a hand on his son's shoulder. He was feeling a surge of protectiveness that he couldn't quite explain.

"This is Beth," Luke said. "Wait—you know her, right? She said you were friends."

"Yeah—" Dan looked up to catch Beth's blue eyes meet his for a fleeting second. "Beth and I were good friends."

"She said you drove a motorcycle on the stage!" Luke said, his face lighting up. "Is that true?"

Dan rolled his eyes in Beth's direction. "Thanks for that, Beth."

"My pleasure." A smile curled her lips.

That had been the one and only time that he'd participated in the pageant, and he'd ended up revving that motorcycle right off the stage and onto a table of poinsettias. That had also been the year he'd asked Beth to marry him. She'd been so pure and untarnished, and he'd been determined to give her the world, if he could. He'd saved his money for months to buy the ring, and at the time it had seemed impressive—the band of gold, a small diamond. Now, looking back, it hadn't been much.

"How'd rehearsal go?" Dan asked.

"Good." Luke nodded. "I'm getting a vest to go with my outfit. So I'll look really elderly."

"Yeah?" Dan chuckled. "And Beth is going to do that?"

He arched an eyebrow in her direction. Last he knew, she couldn't sew.

"I'm only taking measurements," Beth said. "Mrs. Connolly will do the heavy lifting."

She met his gaze, and he felt his expression soften. He broke off eye contact and cleared his throat. Luke was looking at him with that too-sharp gaze he sometimes had—the look that said he understood more than Dan wanted him to.

"We should probably get going," Dan said. "Go find your coat and stuff, Luke."

"Okay." Luke shot Beth a grin. "See you later, old lady."

Dan choked. "Luke!"

"After a while, old-timer," she said with a wink.

Luke headed off to find his stuff, and Dan grimaced and shook his head. "I'm sorry. I've taught him better manners than that."

It mattered to him that Beth know he'd raised his son right. His attempt to hide his past had driven them apart, but at the very least he wanted her to know that he'd done a good job as a parent. He'd certainly sacrificed enough for it.

"Oh, that's just a joke," she said with a shake of her head. "You know…because of his old man costume."

"Yeah…" He'd picked up on that much, but still—Luke knew better. He'd been drilling it into the kid for a couple of years now not to call adults "old." It had been an issue in supermarkets and such, and he'd battled with Luke to get him to use his manners. It probably shouldn't have turned into a power struggle, but it had. So this joke irritated him more than it probably should.

"I'd rather he didn't call adults old," Dan said.

"It was only a joke," she said.

"Beth, I'm his dad—" His tone was sterner

than he'd been aiming for, and he heaved a sigh. A moment ago he'd been feeling protective of her, and now he wanted to tell her to back off. But there was no way to soften that one, so he bit it back.

"Oh." She sobered. "Okay. I will keep that in mind."

Had he offended her? Probably. He was no good with these emotionally charged situations. He never had been. "And I'd rather he not know about our history, if it's all the same to you."

Color tinged Beth's cheeks again, but this time her blue eyes flashed fire. "And you think I'm telling him about that?"

"The motorcycle thing—"

"It was *cute*." Her tone sounded more irritated, though. "I was telling him you'd been in a play, too. Forgive me for telling your son anything about you at all."

"It wasn't cute. It was embarrassing," he retorted. "And that Christmas doesn't exactly hold fond memories for me."

She blinked, and he could tell he'd surprised her. She swallowed, then nodded quickly. Shoot. He'd hurt her. That had been the Christmas that he'd proposed... Was he supposed to think back on those naive days fondly, or something?

"Beth—"

"No, you've made yourself clear." Her eyes misted, and she blinked. "I apologize. I hadn't thought ahead. I thought I was telling him something that would help him connect with you."

"I haven't told him anything about that time," Dan said. Like about the woman who wouldn't marry him when she found out Luke was part of the package. "Anything."

"Got it." She rose to her feet and ran a hand down her belly. "The horrible memories and all that. But you know what? I can remember the happy times. It wasn't all misery and heartbreak just because we didn't last, Dan."

He lowered his voice. "I don't tell him about it because we broke up *because of him.*"

Beth dropped her gaze, and her golden curls swung just enough to hide her expression from his view. He had to explain it all now—there was no going back from this.

"It would crush him, Beth." His voice trembled, and he tried to keep his volume down. "He's already been rejected by his mother, and if he found out that you and I broke up because he came… He's *my* son. You didn't want to be a part of us then, so I call the shots now."

Beth raised her gaze to meet his, and color drained from her face. "He's *yours*. That was clear from the beginning."

"Yeah…" He stopped. Luke *was* his son. That was a biological fact, but he heard the resentment in her tone. "What are you talking about?"

She opened her mouth to answer, just as Luke came running up, his coat open and his feet clunking against the wooden floor in his winter boots. Beth pressed her lips together and looked away. They couldn't talk about this in front of Luke. Not that it mattered. He was frustrated. He needed to clear his head.

"We'd better go," Dan said. "This is a school night."

"See you later, Luke," Beth said, but the good humor was gone from her voice, and Luke seemed to notice. He glanced between his father and Beth.

"Okay, 'bye," Luke said.

Dan turned and walked with his son to-

ward the exit. That could have gone better—
he knew that. He hadn't intended to discuss
those things with Beth at all, but he hadn't
expected her to be here, either.

"Luke," Dan said as they made their way
down the hall toward the outside door.

Luke looked up.

"Don't call people old," Dan said.

"Okay, Dad."

There. Luke needed to know whom to listen to, and Dan wasn't going to share his role
with anyone else, especially not the woman
who'd opted out. Beth could raise her baby
however she liked, but when it came to
Luke—

Dan pushed open the door and followed
Luke out into the chilly night. Dan might not
have always been a great dad, but he'd made
up for lost time. He'd earned the right to call
the shots with Luke with the hard work of
parenting, and Beth, quite frankly, hadn't.

CHAPTER SIX

THE NEXT AFTERNOON, Beth stood in the kitchen next to Granny. Granny was so slender that an apron could just about wrap around her twice, while Beth's apron draped over the front of her belly and she couldn't even do it up behind her.

Granny had woken up lucid from her nap that afternoon. She'd been calm, known the present situation, and hadn't asked for Ralph once. It was like old times, when Beth and Granny would bake together, and her father would go to open the store, his laptop in a bag over his shoulder so that he could type in the quiet moments. Linda would find a way to make herself scarce, and for a couple of hours Beth would feel the comfort of her granny's undivided attention.

This evening, Granny thought it would be a great idea to make some of her famous cinnamon buns, and Beth couldn't turn that down. Granny's cinnamon buns were sticky, gooey and as soft as the inside of a white roll.

"So how are you feeling?" Granny asked.

"Fine."

"I mean, with the baby coming and all the emotions you must be having." Granny pointed to the edge of the dough. "Roll there a little more. Nice and even."

Beth did as she was told. Granny knew cinnamon buns.

"Well?" Granny prodded.

"I'm trying not to feel too much right now. I'm overwhelmed," she admitted. "It's a lot to deal with."

"Hmm." Granny reached over and patted down another edge. "Long strokes with the rolling pin. Long. Longer…"

Beth did as she was told. If she could ever master Granny's recipe, it would be a personal accomplishment. Plus, imagine being able to bake them every time she felt the craving.

"I overstepped with Luke last night," she admitted. "It was completely unintentional, but Danny was mad—like, really mad."

"What did you do?" Granny asked.

"I told Luke a story about Danny when I knew him."

"Ah." Granny chuckled. "That's the thing with parenting. You try to reinvent your past for the benefit of your child, but it never really works."

Would Beth do the same thing for her daughter? Maybe she'd downplay her own stupidity of having a drunken one-night stand, try to cast herself in a better light.

"Danny loves you, still," Granny went on.

In that estimation, Granny might still be out of touch.

"Danny's just trying to figure out how to handle me being back in town," Beth replied with a low laugh. "I've rocked his boat."

But she'd rocked more than Danny. Her pregnancy had left her father off balance, too.

"Granny, how is Dad doing?" Beth asked.

Granny had always had a finger on the pulse of the home, at least before her memory started playing tricks on her. Still, Granny had been here—she'd seen more than Beth had the last few years.

"It's hard for me to tell, dear. I get so confused sometimes..." Granny said after a moment. "I miss out on things now."

"It's okay, Granny," Beth said. She didn't want to put undue pressure on her grandmother. That wasn't fair to her. Beth rubbed a hand over the side of her belly where she felt a foot pressing. Maybe it was better to ask about the past. "Where did we all go wrong?"

"What you wanted and what your father wanted were two different things," Granny said. "You wanted your mother back. That wasn't possible. Your dad wanted someone to grow old with. He wanted a companion, a wife. Anyway, Linda was a very organized person, and your father is not. He's a brilliant writer, but quite a scatterbrain. He was the feeling one, the sensitive one. She was the tough one who kept that shop going."

"Like, the figurative shop, or the actual store?" Beth asked.

"The corner store," Granny replied with a nod.

"But she hardly stepped foot in it!" Beth said.

"Didn't have to. She gave armchair advice. And it worked."

"So if Linda had stayed—"

"She gave up on that store when your father gave up on her."

"Gave up on her, how?" Beth asked.

"He was frustrated with his book—the genius that used to flow so easily seemed dammed up. And he was frustrated with the store because it wasn't making any money. Linda wanted to sell it, and your father saw that as a betrayal. That store was our family's history, but Linda could see that it didn't have a viable future. The more time your father spent in that store, trying to make money by staying open longer, plugging away on the novel that wasn't good enough, the worse it was for their marriage. He turned to the store, and she felt betrayed, too…" Granny sighed. "Marriage isn't easy."

Beth sighed, too, moving that information around in her mind. Funny that so much of what they valued had gone out the door with her stepmother.

"Now for the butter," Granny said, turning back to her mental recipe. "You can never have too much." Granny passed the butter dish. "Don't be shy with it. Dig your fingers in. We'll use up that whole stick."

Beth shot her grandmother a smile. Carbs had been Granny's love language for as long as Beth could remember.

"You seem sad," Beth said quietly.

"I am." Granny nodded. "My son's heart is broken."

Beth smoothed the butter over the soft dough, mulling over her grandmother's revelations. As a teenager, she hadn't thought too much about what it would take for her father and Linda to be happy. She'd assumed that they'd carry on in their selfish love regardless of what it did to her. But they'd broken down over time, and ironically enough, it wasn't because of her, either. It had been over the store that ended up bankrupt regardless.

"What comes after the butter?" Beth asked.

"Next we grill the meat," Granny replied, and Beth shot her a quizzical look.

"What?"

"One pound of ground pork," Granny said. "We will brown it in a pan."

"Granny, we're making cinnamon rolls."

Granny stopped short and frowned. She nodded several times. "Yes, of course. Of course. I know that." She rubbed a hand behind her neck. "Beth, dear, have you seen your grandfather?"

Tears welled in Beth's eyes. Her grandmother's lucidity had been so precious, but never long enough. She'd missed her real Granny so much—the wise woman with insights Beth needed even more now with a baby on the way and her father's personal difficulties. She needed someone on her side.

"Why don't you come tell me how to finish these cinnamon buns?" Beth asked. "I just worked in the butter. I know you add something to the sugar and cinnamon, but I don't know what."

"He's had a cold lately," Granny said. "If he's gone out, I do hope he wore a scarf. That man can be so stubborn."

"Granny, he's—" Beth swallowed the lump in her throat. "He's gone for milk."

Granny frowned and shook her head, then she cast Beth a disapproving look. But she turned back to the counter and peered over Beth's shoulder.

"A sprinkle of salt," Granny said. "It brings out all the flavors."

Beth followed the last of her grandmother's directions, but Granny's heart didn't seem in it anymore. When the cinnamon rolls were in the oven, Beth leaned over and gave Granny a hug.

"These are going to be delicious, Granny," Beth said. "I've been looking forward to your cinnamon buns for so long."

"I think we should bring some to Danny," Granny said.

"No, maybe not a great idea," Beth said. "We're both rather annoyed with each other right now."

"All the more reason to make up, my dear." Granny gave her a pointed look. "You might be upset, but so is he, and your relationship will never work if you don't care for his feelings as tenderly as you care for your own."

Granny was back in the past, and Beth heaved a sigh.

"Maybe in the morning, Granny." Maybe in the morning, Granny would have forgotten.

"I'll go to his house myself," Granny said. "But Danny will have cinnamon buns tonight. It would be appropriate if you were a part of that. Buck up. He's going to be your husband."

Granny's severe look gave Beth pause. She

wasn't going to be distracted so easily, it appeared, and since Granny's mind was in the past, she'd march straight to the house where Danny used to live. It might be easier to just deliver some cinnamon buns.

"Let me call him," Beth said. She didn't have his number, but she did have her phone handy, so she searched the online white pages and came up with a phone number for Daniel Brockwood in North Fork, Alberta.

"Yes, you call him." Granny gave Beth a small smile. "I'm going to my easy chair until the timer goes off."

Beth dialed the number, and it rang three times before he picked up.

"Hello?" Danny sounded tired.

"Hi, Danny, it's me…Beth." She hadn't spoken to him on the phone since they were together, and it felt strange to be doing so now.

"Beth? Is everything okay?"

"Fine." She moved farther away from the doorway that led to the living room. "I'm sorry to disturb you at home. The thing is, Granny and I have been making cinnamon buns, and she's gotten it into her head that you and I need to make up."

"There's no need—"

"Convincing me isn't the problem," Beth interrupted. "She's determined to bring you cinnamon buns, and she's guilting me into being a part of it."

"Ah." Was that a smile she heard in his voice? "Your grandmother does make amazing cinnamon buns. And if they came with a heartfelt apology from you…"

"Danny—" She closed her eyes and grimaced. "I do feel bad for having overstepped with your son—"

"I was joking." His tone softened. "Bring them over. I won't turn down Granny's baking."

"You sure it's okay?" Beth asked cautiously. "She might insist on us…making up."

"I'm sure I can handle it. Besides, she might forget before you get here. Just keep me posted. If she changes her mind, I expect you bring me a peace offering of a fresh cinnamon bun at the store in the morning. You can't get a man's hopes up and then leave him hanging."

"I will. I'm sorry about all of this, Danny."

"Not a problem. Luke's already in bed.

I'm sure we can get through this." His voice was low and warm. "See you in a bit, Beth."

She hung up the phone. It was the small town that made avoiding each other so difficult. Well, the small town and her grandmother's dementia. But Danny was right—she didn't belong in Luke's life. She'd turned down her chance at that a long time ago, and Luke was better off without her.

Except Granny seemed to have other plans when she was locked in the past, and Beth was caught between what was best for a boy and what was best for an old woman. She didn't even have the luxury of considering what was best for herself.

DAN HUNG UP the phone and crossed his arms over his chest. The house was quiet—Luke was asleep, and the TV was on the weather channel with the sound muted. It was almost nine. Dan wasn't sure if Beth and Granny would come that evening or not. If Granny forgot again, they'd all be off the hook. He could only imagine that Beth would breathe a sigh of relief if that happened. It was sad that Granny kept slipping into the past, and a little disconcerting. Dan didn't welcome the chance to revisit old days, because he didn't like who he'd been then. The last five years had changed him in massive, jolting, positive ways. It was like being struck by lightning and coming out stronger than before—a superhero story based on emotional maturity.

Back in the day, he'd been below Beth, and he'd known that. Everyone knew it. Her father was a living literary legend, and the town took great pride in him. The whole country took pride in him. CBC Radio had come to North Fork several times to interview Rick Thomas about his books. Beth's dad had hoped that she would follow in his footsteps, but she'd never been interested in writing like he was. She was more practical, and falling in love with the likes of Dan hadn't been part of her father's plans for her.

More than that, Dan had never seen a functional marriage up close. He was raised by a single father he'd fought with for most of his formative years, and then he'd moved out on his own once he turned seventeen. He'd seen friends fall in love and get married, but that was watching a relationship from the outside. He'd had no idea how a marriage actually worked, and that made for a big inequality in his relationship with Beth. She'd been the one from the "good" family with most of the answers. When a sheltered twenty-five-year-old woman seemed like an emotional guru compared to him, that was probably a bad sign. Now that he'd had five years' space, he could see that he could never have continued that way long-term.

Dan hadn't been ready for marriage—he could see that now. He hadn't liked to talk about his feelings or open up. He preferred to be the tough guy, and it was brawn over brain most times. He used to freeze her out when they argued—a stupid, childish move on his part. And she used to boss him around as if he knew nothing about life because he didn't have the educated influences she'd been raised with. It would have been a mess.

He used to think he was lucky that Lana didn't want him in the picture, and he was also convinced that Lana's rejection absolved him of responsibility toward his son. How much had he missed over those three years? He'd missed Luke's birth and his babyhood. He'd never see his son's first steps or his first tooth. He'd never be able to see a baby in the mall and think, *I remember when Luke was that age.* At the age of twenty-six, he'd had no idea how much he'd regret the choice to run away.

But now, Dan was a different man—stronger, sterner and with a lot more perspective. He liked himself better now, and he no longer felt like he was a rung below Beth Thomas, either. Fatherhood had forced him to face his fears, and as a result, he was twice the man he used to be. He had Luke to thank for that. Given the chance, he would never go back to those days when he and Beth were in love and the world seemed to spin for them alone. Luke had changed his life from shades of gray to startling color.

Dan ambled down the hallway to Luke's bedroom. He opened the door, and the bluish light from his night-light melted out into the hallway. Luke was asleep in a rather uncomfortable-looking position, his head on top of a stuffed toy that would no doubt leave him with a crick in his neck, but Dan had learned the hard way that trying to move him only ruined the kid's rest. He was better off letting Luke sort it out in his sleep.

He sure loved this boy. He could look at that sleeping face and feel a rush of tenderness he'd never known was possible. Dan backed out of the bedroom just as he heard a knock at the front door.

Had they actually come? He wasn't sure if he'd been hoping for that or dreading it. He liked seeing Beth a little too much, and he knew himself—he needed some space to sort that out. Still, his heart beat a little faster at the prospect.

When he opened the door, he wasn't faced with Beth as he expected, but with Granny, Beth standing behind her on the step. They were both in winter jackets, and Granny held a Tupperware container in front of her.

"Hi," Dan said, his gaze slipping past Granny to Beth. Beth's smile looked almost pained, and he chuckled. Granny was going to be a handful tonight, he could already tell. "Come on in."

"Daniel, we have come with cinnamon rolls," Granny said as she stepped inside. "We thought you could use a treat."

Beth came inside behind her grandmother, and Dan shut the door.

"Thanks," he said. "I love your baking, Granny. This *is* a treat."

"Beth made these," Granny replied pointedly. "Didn't you, Beth?"

Beth was obviously being nudged into something here, and Dan cast her an amused smile. He couldn't help but feel a tiny bit let down that the cinnamon buns weren't made by Granny's own hands, because he was convinced that Granny injected magic into her baking. There was no other way to explain it.

"Granny's teaching me the family recipe," Beth said with a small smile, then she mouthed, *Sorry.*

"I'll just go put some frosting on these," Granny said. She bent to take off her boots with surprising agility, then beelined toward Dan's kitchen.

Dan raised an eyebrow. "How did they turn out?"

"They're amazing, thank you." Beth shot him an annoyed look. "And you can stop enjoying this so much. Tomorrow, she'll set up shop in the store again."

"I'm sorry." That was sincere. "I know it's been hard with your grandmother."

Beth nodded, then shrugged. "She was with it for a while today. It was nice—just the two of us in the kitchen, baking. It was like old times when I didn't worry about her wandering off in the snow."

"I'm glad you got that," he said. This slow decline was heartbreaking for all of them.

"And I am sorry about Luke," she went on. "You're right—I'm not a parent yet, and I don't always understand those lines. I'll be more careful from now on."

"Thanks." Dan shrugged. "But you and I are clear that you didn't need to do this... right?"

"Of course!" Beth rolled her eyes. "Granny is the one who's confused. In her mind, we're still engaged and she's saving the wedding. She gave me a rather stern lecture about being more sensitive to your feelings on the way over here."

"Really?" He liked that. "How so?"

"She said that you might put up a tough act, but underneath it all you're a kitten, and that if I don't take care of your feelings, who will?" Beth looked down. "Which is silly, of course, because who takes care of you isn't exactly my business."

"True." He cleared his throat. The thing was, he liked the idea of Beth caring about his feelings for a change.

"And she pointed out that other women would be standing in line for you, and if I didn't treat you right, then someone else would try to scoop you up." She arched one eyebrow and shot him a teasing smile. "Which might very well be true. I wouldn't know."

"Really now?" So Granny was playing the jealousy card, was she? She seemed very serious about her quest to repair their relationship.

"It was quite the lecture." Sadness misted her eyes, and she shrugged. "I'm trying to joke around about it, but this isn't easy for me, Danny."

Playacting for Granny wasn't easy for him, either. Although he and Beth didn't belong together, they did have history that had left his heart in shreds. He'd healed, and he was a different man now, but the reminders were a stab.

"You said something before at the community hall," he said. "Something about Luke being mine. What were you trying to say?"

"Does it even matter?" she asked with a sigh.

"Yeah, it does. To me."

She was silent for a moment, then shrugged. "There wasn't room for me, Danny."

"And you knew that after a day?"

"Luke is your son. There's a biological link there. You looked at him, and you felt it—he was yours in a way he could never be mine."

"We could have tried—"

"Danny, I didn't want to be the Linda in your home." Tears misted her eyes. "And I saw that coming."

That she'd be cold and uncaring? He shook his head. "You saw what, exactly?"

"You'd discovered your son—and that was a powerful moment. You and Luke would always share something special, and I'd be on the outside. And one day, he'd tell me that I wasn't his real mom, and he'd be right. That would hurt, and I'd pull back a bit—to protect myself..." Beth swallowed hard. "I didn't want to slide down into being your Linda, Danny. I couldn't become that."

Dan heard Granny's footfalls behind him, and he glanced back to see her hopeful face. She was a sweet old woman, even if she was living in the wrong year. He appreciated what she thought she was doing—even though it was five years too late.

"I've put the icing on, and the cinnamon buns are covered on your counter," Granny said, folding her hands in front of her. "If you won't eat them until morning, you'll want to pop them in the fridge."

"Thanks," Dan said, but his eyes were fixed on Beth. She didn't want to become like Linda, and he couldn't imagine her getting so tart and inflexible. Yet, she could...

"Have we made up, then?" Granny asked.

"Yes, Granny, it's all sorted out," Beth said with a small smile. "You can rest easy tonight."

"Daniel?" Granny gave him a questioning look.

"All sorted out," Dan echoed hollowly. But it wasn't.

"I'm very glad to hear it," Granny said earnestly. "There are people who would be thrilled to see you two fail. Don't give them the satisfaction. Now, would you hug or something?" Granny gestured toward them like the director of a play. "Kiss and make up, perhaps? Come now, you'll both feel better."

Beth looked from her grandmother to Dan in shock, and Dan felt a wave of worry. Granny was taking this all the way, it seemed. How far were they willing to go to appease a confused old lady?

Beth licked her lips. "Granny, I'm sure we can just go home now..."

"I'm not some old prude. Now make up properly or it won't stick." Granny gestured toward them again. "Come on. Best learn this now before the wedding, because married people have to make up plenty. Trust me on that."

There wasn't going to be any way to get around this and get Granny calmly home, he could tell. So he put a hand on Beth's shoulder, and she looked up at him, stricken.

"You ready?" he murmured.

"For what?" she whispered.

Dan bent down and gathered her into his arms. She felt different than she had in the past. Her could feel the swell of her belly, and what felt like a gentle kick from within. Had he felt that? He wasn't even sure. But he wrapped his arms around her and leaned his cheek against her silken hair. It felt better than he'd imagined it would, and his heart softened in his chest. She smelled of baking and something soft and womanly that he couldn't quite identify. Beth's hands moved around his waist and they stood there for a few beats, their hearts thumping against each other in a calming rhythm.

"There." Granny sounded pleased. "See? It makes it stick."

She was probably right—the simple act of pulling someone close had a way of disintegrating the last of the anger. Except he and Beth weren't a couple any longer.

Dan released her and stood up straight again. Beth looked a little rumpled, and she smoothed her coat down once more before giving Dan a shy smile.

"We'd better get going," Beth said.

"Okay." Only the two of them knew how much they were willing to do for Granny. By tomorrow, Granny wouldn't remember much of this, he was sure. "And thanks for the cinnamon rolls."

Beth and Granny did their coats back up, and he noticed a spot of pink in Beth's cheeks when she glanced at him. It had been a nice hug, he realized. Maybe she felt the same way. It had been a long time since he'd held her in his arms, and he missed it—the closeness, the connection.

"Good night," Beth said, and she stepped outside. Granny followed, and when the old woman looked back at him, he thought he saw a more knowing look in those glittering blue eyes than usual. She was a complicated old lady.

He watched from the door as they got into their car, then he shut the door. He stood there in the living room feeling strangely peaceful. A hug—was that what he'd been longing for all this time? It hadn't been all bad back then…when Beth had to wrap her arms around him and he'd inhaled that soft, feminine scent of her skin so close to his. He missed that.

Dan sighed and headed toward the kitchen. There was a pan of cinnamon buns waiting, and he had plans to eat a couple of them before morning. Granny's baking deserved his full attention.

CHAPTER SEVEN

THE NEXT MORNING, Beth was still thinking about that oddly tender hug in Danny's living room. She still fit under his chin—somehow, she'd wondered if she still would with all this tummy. She'd been a little nervous that he wouldn't be able to make it work, a reflection of her own physical discomfort lately. She felt huge, so unlike her usual self. Her figure wouldn't be the same after this, and she had no idea how she felt about that.

But Dan had managed to wrap his arms around her without any difficulty—he'd just leaned down and gathered her up in those strong arms of his, and pregnant or not, she still fit.

And yet, just before that hug, she'd been opening up more than she'd wanted to, telling him her fear of becoming just like Linda. She shouldn't have said anything—it didn't help—but it felt good to talk to him again.

She'd always been completely honest with Danny, and she'd believed that he'd been the same with her until that was proven wrong. That hug had been more emotional than she'd wanted to admit, and she'd liked the feel of his strong chest against her cheek, the sensation of his heart beating steadily. Dan was bigger now—bulkier, and definitely stronger. And his arms closing around her as she shut her eyes and absorbed that unique musky scent of his had reminded her of just how much she'd missed this.

That hug had been fake, though—prodded by a meddling old lady—and it was the kind of soothing intimacy Beth could not allow herself to enjoy, because it wasn't real. Right now, with a baby on the way and the fears of delivery mounting, she wished she had a husband by her side, hugging her when she needed reassurance, doing cake runs when she got cravings…but she didn't, and wishing wasn't helpful.

Beth came into the kitchen to find her father at the table with a mug of coffee. He was dressed as if he were going to work at the store—a button-up shirt and a pair of khaki pants—but he wasn't, obviously. Just sitting there with his coffee beside him and his laptop open on the kitchen table.

"Morning," Rick said. "How'd you sleep?"

"Not too badly." She paused and gave her father a smile. "Are you writing, Dad?"

"Job hunting." He took a sip from his mug.

Of course. He'd need to find something to replace the store, but the image of her father looking for work was a hard one to swallow. He didn't deserve to be in this position, not after how hard he'd worked all those years, not after he'd established himself as a literary voice for the country.

"I'd rather hear you were working on your book," she said.

"Doesn't pay enough," he said. "I have a granddaughter on the way, remember?"

So this was on her...but not entirely. The store's failure hadn't been her fault, and she knew better than to take everything he said to heart.

"Do you miss the store, Dad?" she asked.

Her father sucked in a breath, then nodded. "Yeah, I do. I grew up there. Like you did. I worked side by side with my dad in that shop up until the day he died. You could say I miss it."

"Have you gone to see it?" she asked.

Rick shook his head. "Can't bring myself to, Beth."

She knew that the shop now belonged to Danny, but while the contents were being sorted out, it felt like it still belonged to them a little bit, too. None of them were ready to say goodbye to the family store, but life had a way of grinding on whether a person was ready for it or not.

"Have you found much else there that we'll want to keep?" her father asked after a moment.

"The triple frame with our pictures in it that I gave to Linda," Beth said.

Her father nodded, but he didn't say anything.

"There might be more little treasures, Dad. I'll make sure we don't lose anything."

"Thanks." He took another sip of coffee. "I appreciate it, Beth."

Her father couldn't bear to see the store emptied out, and Beth was having trouble staying away. It was loyalty, mostly, because Danny only made her feel more unsettled. She was still attracted to him, but she knew better than to let emotions get involved. She might be back in North Fork, but she wasn't the same woman who'd left. So when she visited that store, it was because it had been a family hub, a touchstone for their memories. It was *that*, she told herself, not Danny.

That morning, Beth put on her winter coat and trudged out toward the old store. Danny had said that he wanted to have it cleared out by Christmas, and a couple of weeks after that, Beth's daughter was due to be born. Everything would be different in the new year, and they'd all just have to move on.

The store was unlocked, and Beth stepped inside to find Danny breaking down cardboard boxes.

"Hi," Beth said, and she headed toward the space heater.

"So how was Granny this morning?" Danny asked.

"She forgot everything," Beth replied with a small smile. "Almost makes your sacrifices seem in vain, doesn't it?"

"That wasn't a sacrifice. I've wanted to do that since you arrived."

Beth blinked, then dropped her gaze.

"I thought I was enemy number one for you," she said, glancing up.

"Oh, you are." He shot her an impish smile. "But you seemed like you could use a hug. That's all. I think you've had a rough time."

And she had needed that human connection—Danny hadn't been wrong there. But right now, she also needed to be self-sufficient. She wasn't used to going it alone, but this was her new reality.

Danny sliced a box open with his cutter, then dropped the knife on the countertop while he flattened the cardboard.

"What about Luke?" she asked. "What if he'd seen that?"

Danny dropped the box into a pile. "He was asleep, and that kid sleeps like a log."

"Oh…" What did she know about sleeping children? Danny grabbed another box, then paused. He licked his lips, then looked up at her, and she could see apology in his face.

"I just wanted Granny to stay calm," Danny said. "I didn't mean to make you uncomfortable or anything."

"No, it's fine." It was more than fine, and she was trying to forget about how nice it had felt.

"With our history—" Danny shrugged.

"Never seeing each other again would have been easier, I suppose."

Beth felt a stab at those words. He was happy to hug her because she looked like she needed it, but he'd rather never see her again?

"North Fork is my home, too," she retorted. She might not feel like she fit in the same way, but when she needed somewhere to come to, somewhere to have her baby, North Fork was here. Her father was here.

"I know." Danny shook his head. "Maybe that came out wrong. It's just—we almost got married, Beth. That's huge. We had a wedding planned and ready to go. Flowers, dress, the works. After almost marrying a woman, it's hard to go back to a casual hello in the street. I don't wish you ill, Beth, I just don't know how to do this balancing act."

This was awkward—even more so since he was taking over her family's store. There was nothing easy about their relationship, but small towns were like that. People had history together, and then they had to be able to find a new way to relate, because avoiding someone in a place this size wasn't remotely possible.

"You act like my heart wasn't broken, too," she said.

"You're the one who walked away." Danny tossed the cardboard onto the pile.

"In my defense, you'd just dumped a pretty big surprise on me," she countered.

"Luke was a shock for me, too!" He turned toward her, all the gentleness out of his expression now.

"It's not nearly the same," Beth shot back. "You knew he existed, at least! You just didn't know that his mom was going to do that!"

Danny winced, and she immediately regretted the words. What good was this going to do? It was five years ago, and they'd both moved on. What were they doing?

"I needed—" Danny stopped, then shook his head. "Forget it."

He'd always done that—come within a hair of saying what was really on his mind and then backed off. She'd always won their arguments, but it had never felt like a win. She'd hated it, because she had wanted to know what he was feeling, and he'd stayed bottled up.

"You needed what?" she asked, her tone more annoyed than she wanted.

"I needed some understanding," he said, dark gaze snapping to hers. "I needed you to see it from my perspective. And if you still didn't want to marry me, I could have lived with that. But you didn't stop to see what it meant to *me*."

Beth undid the last of her coat buttons, her mind going over that night. Granted, she'd been focused on herself. Danny had hidden something massive from her, and she was supposed to roll with that? She'd been scared, upset, betrayed... And all her father's warnings that Danny wouldn't be able to give her the life she wanted had come back in a flood. She *couldn't* marry Danny—not like that.

"I was freaked out," Beth said. "We'd talked about what our life would be like together, and you'd never even hinted that there was a child out there who might come knocking...or an ex-girlfriend you might owe child support to."

"I know." Danny grabbed another box and used more force than necessary to tear it apart. Their arguments had normally been like this—her outtalking him and him simmering. But they weren't a couple anymore. They were neighbors, that was it. Maybe it was time to put an end to these stupid patterns already.

"But you said I didn't see it from your perspective," she said, softening her tone. "So… what was it like for you?"

He stopped manhandling the box, and a couple of beats of silence passed. Then he said, "I was facing my responsibilities. I dreaded telling you, because you were already taking a step down to be with me. I knew you'd be upset, and believe me, I never wanted to disappoint you. For the first time of my life, I was manning up."

"Fessing up, you mean," she said.

"Figuring out how to support my son!" The ice was back in his tone again. "I get that it was a shock. I get that I should have told you long before. I was scared, too. I didn't know how I was going to raise Luke, but I was damn well going to try!"

"Wait—" She put her hands up. "What do you mean, I took a step down to be with you?"

"Didn't you?"

"No." She frowned. "Is that what you thought? You were more street-smart than I was. I was more bookish. We balanced each other out."

"That's not what your dad thought."

"Who cares what my dad thought?" she shot back.

"You did."

Danny bent and gathered up the boxes, then strode to the front door. He used his boot to kick the door open and then disappeared out into the cold, leaving a swirl of snowy air in his wake. Beth stood there for a moment, the blast of cold air pushing against her legs. Her heart pounded in her chest, but she stood alone in front of the space heater, her rejoinders packed like a ball in her throat. She knew she'd hurt Danny, but she'd been hurt, too. She'd had to walk away from their wedding, as well, and it wasn't because she was heartless or spoiled. She'd had reasons, and those reasons weren't that she was a cut above him.

The door opened again, and Danny came striding back inside.

"I wasn't the bad guy you made me out to be," he said, picking up where he'd left off. "And you could have left me, Beth, but you didn't have to paint me as the horrible man who'd broken your heart, because that wasn't the whole story, either. You left because of *you*! I needed you then, Beth. It isn't only the women who need support in relationships. Meeting my son for the first time—having him suddenly thrust into my home—was the hardest, scariest thing of my life, and when I called you to come over, I needed your support. I needed you to stand with me, Beth, but instead you took off because you couldn't handle it." He was trembling now, and she jumped as he slapped a hand down on the counter. "Well, that's life! Sometimes it's hard, and that's why there are wedding vows! You walked out on me when I needed you, so don't act like I was a monster who ruined your life. I had every right to expect that you'd stand by me—that's what marriage *is*!"

THE DOOR STOOD open still, and Dan slammed it shut behind him, cutting off the winter wind. He and Beth stared at each other in uncomfortable silence. He immediately regretted everything he'd just said. He'd told himself he wouldn't do this—get into their old business all over again. But he'd had it bottled up for so long that when he loosened that cap, it all just came rushing out.

"You're right." Her voice was quiet, but it stopped him short. Was she actually agreeing with him? He hadn't seen that one coming.

"What?" His voice was still gruff from emotion, and he turned to face her.

Her chin trembled ever so slightly. "I left you because I couldn't handle it. It was too much. I wanted a sweet husband who would build a life with me and have all those firsts with *me*, not someone else."

"Okay, then." Had he just won this round? He wasn't even sure. "I wasn't with Lana for any of it, though," he added. "She dumped me a month after she took the pregnancy test."

"I know…" She shook her head. "But you say that marriage is standing with each other, facing the hard stuff together…and you're right. But marriage is also being open and honest with each other. You expected me to embrace being a stepmom to a child I had never heard of before, marry you and just figure it all out later? How could I ever be sure that was your only secret?"

He'd lost her trust—he could see that, and he knew he only had himself to blame.

"You could have stayed. We could have talked. We could have put the wedding off for a few weeks. There were other options!"

"I know it was harsh," she said. "But I grew up with a stepmother. I made her as miserable as possible, and she finally reached her limit with me. The thing is, I can't claim to be a better woman. I think Linda tried the big heart thing at first." Beth sucked in a deep breath. "She took me to get my nails done after they got back from the honeymoon. And she took me clothes shopping. She called it a girls' day out."

Dan stayed silent, waiting for her to go on. She looked away, swallowing hard. When she started talking again, he could hear the regret in her voice. "I told her that her breath smelled, even after she brushed her teeth, and that maybe she should see a doctor about it." Beth's cheeks tinged pink. "I still remember the look on her face, like I'd punched her or something. Then she just closed off."

Ouch. Dan dragged a hand through his hair.

"And I'm not proud of that," Beth went on. "But what I'm saying is, there's a stepfamily dynamic, and while I could have made different choices than Linda did, did I really want to take all of that on? Linda didn't like me and I didn't like her. She wedged me away from my dad because he was forced to constantly choose sides, and he always chose Linda's."

"He was trying to stay married, I guess," Dan said.

"Very likely," Beth agreed. "They maintained a united front, if nothing else. Still, I wasn't entirely innocent, either, so when I look back on all that I put Linda through, I have to ask myself if it's worth it. If you know that it's going to come with a whole heap of heartache, why not avoid that altogether?"

Dan felt those last words like a kick to the gut. It had been five years, and it shouldn't hurt that much, but it did. *He* wasn't worth the challenge of raising Luke together.

"So you didn't love me enough," he said, his voice low. It was better to know that now.

"I did love you enough! I didn't *trust* you enough!" She pulled a hand through her hair.

"You'd already told me how many lies to cover up the fact that you had a child, and I was supposed to trust that you'd be mature enough to both parent this little boy and be a supportive husband to me?"

"Fair enough," he said. There was really nothing more to say.

"Besides, Lana made it very clear what my life would be like," Beth added, and he caught a slight quiver in her voice. Did the thought of Lana still bother her?

"Lana was just mad I was getting married," Dan said. "She was jealous of you. She was a single mom, and I was the screwup who'd gotten her pregnant. I wasn't supposed to be the one who landed a sweet girl and got married."

"She was tougher than me." Beth shrugged.

"I'll give you that," he agreed.

"And she vowed to be in our life for all eternity..." Beth sighed. "You're right. I didn't have the thick skin or the attitude to take her on."

Lana had been a regular force to be reckoned with. She'd been tough and mouthy, but most of the girls in his old neighborhood had been that way. He'd learned to look beneath the bravado, but he could see why a woman like Beth would have been intimidated.

"It was only because she had so much less than you did," he tried to explain.

"Maybe so," Beth agreed. "But that was a lot for me to take on."

"Yeah, I know..." Dan sighed. "Lana could be a real handful, but when she dropped Luke off at my place, I got to see what motherhood had changed her into."

Beth glanced up. "What was she like?"

"Tired, mostly." Dan's heart welled with sadness at the memory. "She wasn't quite so tough anymore, either. I mean, she looked very much like a mom."

Lana had sat in his living room with her hands clutched in front of her in a white-knuckled grip, and she'd asked him to please take their son for a while. She desperately needed a break. Her clothes were old, and her purse looked a bit ratty. She smelled of cigarette smoke and a bit of weed.

"And she just walked away from him?" Beth asked quietly.

"Luke was asleep," Dan said, his mind

running over the details of that night. "Remember, he was only three. We laid him on the couch, and I put a blanket over him. She looked at him for a long time, and then she kissed him—" A lump rose in his throat. "She said he liked grilled cheese, and then she kissed him again and almost ran out the door…"

Tears misted Beth's eyes, and she blinked it back. "I can't imagine," she whispered.

She probably couldn't, Dan realized. Beth had had a stepmother, but she'd also had a clean home, a supportive family, new clothes and friends. Her stepmother had been lacking, but the rest of her support network had been solid. When Beth got pregnant, she had a family to help support her and a town that would get behind her. Lana hadn't been so lucky. And that was what had attracted him to Lana to begin with—she'd understood his background.

"Lana was overwhelmed," Dan said. "She didn't think she could handle being a mom anymore. She said she had no patience and she yelled all the time. She was afraid she'd start hitting him. She'd been abused when she was a kid, and it turned out that it was pretty easy to keep the cycle going."

Dan still remembered that little pile of kid stuff she'd unloaded from her car—a car seat, some clothes, a blanket, a tattered teddy bear, a few plastic toys, half a bag of blue training pants and bottle of Coke. It had taken Dan months to wean the kid off caffeinated drinks, and Luke's baby teeth had suffered for it.

"But she just left—" Beth seemed to be stuck on that part. She was cradling her belly protectively.

"Yeah," he said with a nod. "She just left."

"Any woman that would—"

"No!" Dan swallowed hard. "Beth, don't do that. It's easy to judge someone when you've had every other privilege. She didn't want to leave him, I know that."

Beth nodded. "But you said before that you were scared she'd come back. If she didn't want to leave him…"

She let the implied question hang in the air. If Beth wasn't allowed to judge Lana's actions, what about him? He'd obviously been doing some judging of his ex.

"Okay, yeah," Dan said with a shrug. "She

didn't want to leave him, but she did. We exchanged phone numbers and addresses, and she's kept me updated so I know where to find her if I need to. Right now, she's in Vancouver."

"And you're afraid she'll come for him," Beth concluded.

"I am." Dan sighed. "It's different for you. You don't have to worry about the father breezing back in and demanding anything. Lana's never been predictable. So it's complicated."

"I'm sorry, Dan." Beth pulled her hair out of her face, and she looked like the same old Beth again with those big blue eyes and the pink in her cheeks.

"For what?" he asked with a sad smile.

"For all of it. You didn't ask for this."

The one thing he'd asked for—Beth's hand in marriage—hadn't panned out, either. But he still wouldn't go back if he had the chance.

"I might not have asked for it," Dan said, "but it made me grow up. I'm the man I am today because of all the hard stuff. And if you'd stayed with me, we'd have grown into it together."

It wasn't easy, and there were challenges. She would have felt like a failure some days and exulted in a new victory on other days. She would have gone through all the things he did—feeling lonely and other times desperate for a few hours without someone pestering her. She would have messed up—a lot. She would have felt pride and guilt and love all wrapped up together in one heart-crushing emotion. They would have staggered through all those firsts and growing pains together, and they would have been better for it. She wasn't escaping the experience, either—she was about to do it all on her own with her baby.

Beth was silent for a moment, then she stepped closer and put out her hand. "I'm sorry I couldn't do it."

He took her cool, soft fingers into his rough palm, and he stood there, angry, tired, scraped out.

"And I hope I'll be able to say the same thing about my own daughter a few years from now," she added.

Maybe Dan and Beth hadn't been meant for marriage. Maybe they'd make better friends as they navigated single parenthood a few blocks apart. But she was back now, and they couldn't just melt into casual acquaintances.

"You'll be okay, Beth," he said, and he took a step closer. He looked down at her pale fingers, and he longed to lift them to his lips. What was wrong with him? He was supposed to be over her...

"Are *we* okay?" Beth asked, looking up at him. She was close enough that he could have bent down and kissed her, and he tried to push the thought back.

"You mean, are we friends?" Dan asked, his voice catching.

"Something like that." She looked up in that moment, and her lips parted as she sucked in a wavering breath. Dan pushed aside all those reasons for keeping his distance, slid a hand behind her neck and bent down so that his lips hovered over hers. She didn't speak, but she didn't pull away, either. Then he closed the distance and his lips met hers. They were fuller than before, softer, and his mouth moved over hers, his heart aching for all they'd lost. They could have been something...

She pulled back, and he released her. It was for the best—he knew that.

"Sorry," he whispered.

"Danny, we can't—" She stopped, swallowed.

"I know," he said huskily. "That was… sorry. I shouldn't have." He was still drawn to her in powerful ways—the very reason he'd proposed to begin with. She was the one woman who stirred his blood like this, who softened his heart, who made him willing to cross oceans for her. But she hadn't been willing to do the same for him, and now everything was different.

Beth stepped back and moved toward the door. He'd freaked her out. Great. That hadn't been the plan, but then neither had kissing her.

"I'm going to go," she said, and she pulled her coat closer around her and opened the door.

"Beth—"

She disappeared as the door swung shut behind her, and Dan shut his eyes and muttered an oath. What would he have said? Nothing. He wasn't meaning to toy with her.

He'd crossed a line, and that couldn't happen again. They both knew why they couldn't work, and he was playing with fire.

CHAPTER EIGHT

THAT KISS HAD shaken Beth, and she'd been thinking about it ever since it happened the day before. Danny shouldn't have done it—but then, she should have stopped him. They were both culpable there. What was she thinking? She had a baby on the way, and whatever she'd felt for Danny five years ago had no business coming back now.

She knew this. So why hadn't she been able to step back when he'd bent over her, his dark gaze moving over her face, his breath tickling her lips? He'd been waiting for her to stop him—she knew that. And she hadn't.

Beth stood in the kitchen, absently munching on a bowl of trail mix. Her father stood in front of the open fridge, gazing into its depths. He'd said something, and she'd missed it.

"Sorry, Dad. What's that?"

"We should go tonight," Rick said, pulling out a carton of eggs.

"Where?"

"The tree-lighting ceremony. We always went when you were a kid. It would be nice."

The park by the church already glowed with colored Christmas lights on every tree except the central spruce. It was a massive tree that took the local fire truck and its ladder to decorate, and the tree-lighting ceremony was an exciting night for the town. There was free hot cocoa and a visit from Santa, and a collection was taken up for the North Fork Food Bank.

A lovely evening, to be sure, but Beth wasn't in the mood. She was used to living alone in Edmonton, and now she was sharing the house with her father and grandmother. What she really wanted right now was a night to herself, and for everyone else go without her. She needed to think, to process. She needed to get her emotions in order so that she wouldn't find herself kissing Danny again.

"That's okay, Dad," she said. "I'd rather stay in."

Besides, she had personal memories at-

tached to that park. It was at the tree-lighting
ceremony six years ago that Danny had proposed. He'd tugged her away from the crowd,
behind a tree, and pulled out that little velvet box. His eyes had been full of pleading,
and she could still remember the words he
spoke: *I love you, Beth. So much. I just want
to get married...*

The ring was a simple band and the stone
was small, but it had been so beautiful to her.
It was a little too big, but she hadn't cared,
and she'd refused to get it sized, because it
would mean taking it off again.

"Your granny wants to go," Rick replied,
heading to the stove and letting the fridge
close behind him. "Besides, I have my little
girl home again for the first time in ages.
Remember how you and I used to watch that
tree light up when you were small? You'd
sit on my shoulders and get hot cocoa in my
hair."

Beth smiled. Yes, she did remember that—
vaguely. There were pictures in the family
album of Rick pulling Beth and Michael on
a sled through the park, and their mother
holding hot cocoa in her mittened hands with
that beautiful smile of hers... Beth also re-

membered how their family enjoyment of the Christmas tree lighting had changed once Linda came into the picture. Instead of Rick standing close to his kids, he'd been holding hands with Linda, Linda's head on his shoulder, and Beth and Michael standing off with their friends. Beth had said she preferred it that way, but that was a lie. She'd wanted her dad's attention, for him to take some joy in her for a change. But her father had seemed happy enough with Linda, so—

"Come on," Rick coaxed. "It'll be fun. Hot cocoa…Santa… It's Christmas, Beth!"

Her dad needed this, she could tell. He'd had a rough year, too, and this Christmas he seemed to be harkening back to those seasons when her mom was alive and they'd all been happy. Before their hearts had all been broken, and before Linda.

"All right," she agreed. "For you."

Besides wanting some quiet, she knew that avoiding every reminder of Danny wouldn't be possible, either. She'd have to start some new traditions with her own daughter and push those old memories far into the past where they belonged. Maybe she could start that process tonight.

"Great." Her father grinned. "Omelet?"

After a supper of omelets and peanut butter sandwiches, Beth, Rick and Granny ventured out into the night. The park was walking distance from their home, and considering the number of people who would be driving into town, trying to navigate the parking didn't make sense.

When they arrived at the park, they stopped by the hot chocolate table and each got a foam cup filled with frothy cocoa. One large marshmallow floated on the top of Beth's, and she took a scalding sip. It was as good as she remembered. There was no skimping on the Christmas cocoa in North Fork. It was made with whole milk, melted dark chocolate and as many marshmallows as would fit on top.

"I need two, please," Granny said to the teenage girl who was serving.

"Why do you need two?" Beth asked.

"One for your grandfather, dear," Granny replied patiently, and she held up two gloved fingers for the girl's benefit.

Beth sighed. This would be awkward, and Granny would likely spill hot cocoa on herself and get burned, or chilled, or just sticky.

They couldn't let her wander the park looking for her late husband.

"Why don't I hold Grandpa's cocoa," Beth said. "I'll give it to him when I see him."

"Will you?" Granny looked perplexed. "All right. Thank you, Beth." Beth took one of the cups, which left her hands full.

"Granny, let's go watch the kids sit on Santa's knee," Rick said, shooting Beth a tight smile. They all knew their job here— get rid of the second cocoa and distract Granny.

Other patrons had lined up for the hot chocolate table, and Beth took a step back to make room for a boisterous family with several eager kids.

"Beth?" The voice behind her was low and deep, and she recognized it immediately. She turned to see Danny and Luke. She felt the heat come to her face—the last time she'd seen him he'd been kissing her in the store… She licked her lips and held out the extra cup of cocoa.

"Hot chocolate?" Beth asked.

Luke took the cup and grinned, then took a noisy slurp.

"Granny ordered two," Beth said. She and

Danny exchanged a look, and she could see the apology in his eyes.

"Look, about yesterday—" Danny looked down at his son, then stopped. "We're on our way to see Santa right now. Why don't you walk with us?"

"I'm not sitting on his knee," Luke said with an eye roll. "I'm not a baby."

"So stand beside him in a manly way," Danny retorted. "I'm taking a picture, regardless." Danny glanced back at Beth. "Come along?"

Luke might think he was too old, but he still seemed a tad excited to see Santa. Beth fell into step beside Danny as they walked through the crunching snow. Luke walked far enough ahead to afford them a little privacy.

"About yesterday," Danny said quietly. "I shouldn't have done that."

"Why did you?" she asked suddenly. "I mean, I'm huge right now—"

"You're still gorgeous." He glanced down at her. Heat rose in her face. "Okay, in all honesty—" He paused, seeming to gather his thoughts. "I know it won't work with us, Beth. I get that. There's just this part of me that still reacts to you like I used to. But I can control that. I'm a grown man."

She nodded. "Okay." There was a part of her that was reacting to him in the same way—melting under his touch. And she didn't need any lectures on why it wouldn't work between them, either.

"I'm serious," he added. "I'll keep that in check."

She shot him a small smile, and they fell into silence as they passed an ice sculpture display.

"Do you still come every year?" Beth asked after a moment.

Danny's expression turned wistful, then he shrugged. "It's different when you have a kid. You'll see."

She'd forgotten how nice it felt to walk with Danny. He made cold nights feel safer, just because he was there. She'd have to get over that.

"I didn't want to come," she admitted.

"Have I ruined the park for you?" he asked. Was he remembering the night he proposed, too?

"A little," she admitted. Was that cruel to say? They slowed their pace, Luke still well in sight. She didn't seem to have to explain what she meant—Danny had been there, too, hadn't he? They'd excitedly made their wedding plans, and no matter how hard Beth tried, she'd never been able to eclipse those sweet, first-love memories with anyone else.

"It gets better. Look at Luke," Danny said. "He sees the magic—the lights, the hot chocolate, the Christmas carols… This is new for him. He's making his own memories, and one day he'll get his heart broken, I'm sure. It happens to the best of us, but I'm doing my best to make sure he's got a pile of happy memories to fall back on. You'll do the same thing with your daughter. You had a pile of happy childhood memories of your own. Us—whatever we had—will get covered over eventually, and you'll make different memories here."

Beth breathed in the winter air and looked around at the parents pulling their kids on sleds, the skaters holding hands as they sliced along the flooded track, the crackle of the central bonfire… Not too far in the future, she'd have a little girl running at her side, and Beth would be watching Riley experience these traditions for the very first time, too. But that was hard to imagine.

Santa was ahead, and Luke got into line with the other kids. They stopped a few yards away, and Danny's coat brushed her arm. She was tempted to lean into his strength, but that was an old habit. She sipped her hot chocolate instead and watched as a toddler started to cry on Santa's knee.

"That first Christmas after you left," Danny went on, "I brought Luke here for the tree-lighting ceremony. He let go of my hand for just a second, and when I looked down, he was gone. I looked everywhere for him, and about twenty minutes later, there was an announcement over the loudspeaker that they'd found a little boy, and I went to collect him."

Beth shook her head. "You must have gone nuts."

"I just about cried when I picked him up again," Danny said. "I didn't know I could feel like that. But that's when I realized that I'd make new memories, and they'd be intense, too. So when I look at that tree over there, I remember you." Danny leaned over and nudged her arm with his, and her gaze swept toward the spot where he'd pulled out that velvet box. "That can't be helped. And when I look at the skating circle," Danny went on, "I remember shouting Luke's name and looking everywhere, and realizing every single boy was wearing a gray snowsuit, and feeling sick to my stomach."

"Are you still traumatized?" she asked softly.

"A little," he admitted. "Welcome to parenthood."

But she understood what he meant. They'd have more memories, more life, more heartbreak and panic, joy and heart-melting love with their kids. Life would plod on, and one day this park wouldn't be the place where Danny had proposed anymore—it would be just the park again.

One day. He had a bit of a head start on that.

Luke moved up in line, and a few more kids got behind him. She noticed how Danny's gaze didn't leave Luke for long, his vigilance silent and stable. And then Beth saw her father through the crowd. Granny was beside him, rapturously watching the kids get their photos taken with Santa.

Rick's gaze was on Beth, his expression sad and full of regret, but she could only guess what exactly her dad regretted most. Another watchful father—a few years too late.

DAN LOOKED DOWN at Beth by his side.

"So are we okay?" he asked uncertainly.

"We're fine." She gave him a small smile, but he caught the glimmer of forgiveness in her eye. They were both different people now, and maybe there were still some sparks, but he knew what was realistic and what wasn't. They were better off as friends, and he wouldn't let himself go there again.

"Luke's at the front," Dan said, nodding to the lineup. "I'd better go snap that picture."

"Go," she said with a low laugh. "You might not get another one next year. I'll go see my family."

Dan looked over to where Rick and Granny stood, aglow in the rosy light of the tree next to them. "Okay," he said. "I'll see you."

Dan passed the waiting parents getting to the front for a good picture, and Beth moved away, too. Different memories—that was the point, right? Except he still felt an ache when he thought about her. This park didn't hold the same meaning that it used to, but that didn't mean that Beth hadn't hollowed out a part of his heart that had never fully healed. Kids changed a lot of things—they certainly changed what was possible now—but they couldn't erase everything. He wouldn't tell her that, though.

Dan turned his attention to his son. Luke used to cling to Dan's hand when he was smaller, dancing from one foot to the other in the excitement of seeing Santa. Not anymore. He stood in line by himself now and wanted a bit of independence. Kids grew up faster than Dan had realized.

Dan pulled out his phone and took a few snaps as Luke stood next to Santa's chair. He didn't sit on his lap, but Luke did lean over and they exchanged a few words. Santa looked perplexed, then put a finger on the side of his nose. When Luke moved away and made room for the next kid, Dan met him at the other side.

"Want to see the pictures?" Dan asked. He turned his phone around so Luke could see.

"Yeah." Luke sounded a little too encouraging, like this was more for Dan than for him.

"What did you ask Santa for this year?" Dan asked.

"Santa's not real, Dad," Luke said. "That's Mr. Henderson from the grocery store."

"I don't know about that," Dan said, glancing back. "Because I just saw Mr. Henderson by the hot cocoa."

A fib, obviously, but a fib in the hopes of renewing a little Christmas spirit.

"You didn't…did you?" Luke looked back.

"What did you ask for?" Dan repeated.

"For Mom." Luke's words were almost too quiet to hear, and a lump rose in Dan's throat. For all his attempts to make memories Luke could look back on with happiness, there was still a part of the boy's heart that longed for the mother he couldn't remember.

"Do you want to talk?" Dan asked, stopping short and touching his son's shoulder.

"Nope."

"Well, I do. What did Santa say to that?" Dan might have a bone to pick with Al Henderson at the grocery store later.

"He said he couldn't make any promises, but he understood," Luke replied.

Good answer, Dan thought bitterly. He didn't have a better one.

"Son, if I could fix all of this for you, I would," Dan said quietly. "But I can't. You just have to trust that I'm doing my absolute best to give you everything in my power. I told you before that I can't bring your mom back into your life right now, but that doesn't mean we won't be able to make this work in a few years."

"That's too far away," Luke muttered.

"It feels far," Dan admitted. "I know. But it isn't really. On my end of things, it passes by in a blink."

"Well, at my end it's super long!" Luke retorted.

What was he supposed to do—call up Lana and let Luke get his heart broken all over again? What if she didn't come see him? What if she came to see him, and he didn't get the love from her that he longed for? What if she decided to try again with him and took off with Luke for Vancouver? It was all fine and good to have the law on his side, but a whole lot could happen to a kid for the few weeks it took to find him. The thought chilled his blood.

"You just gotta trust me, Luke." It was all Dan had.

He stood there, frustrated. He wished this was easier, or at least outlined for him. First you do this, then that. But there were no steps to follow to fix a situation like this one. He looked over to where Beth stood next to her father, and he heaved a sigh. He'd been avoiding Rick Thomas ever since he'd started the process of buying that piece of property, not that he'd be able to do it forever.

"We'd better go over and say hi to Rick," Dan said.

"That guy doesn't like you," Luke said. Out of the mouths of babes.

"Don't worry about that, Luke. He'll come around." He sounded more sure than he felt, which was a good thing right now. Dan dug a ten-dollar bill out of his pocket. "Why don't you go put this into the money box for the food bank."

Luke took the cash and headed off toward the decorated box, and Dan turned his steps toward where the Thomas family stood. *He'll come around.* Would he? If Dan was about to be verbally abused by Rick Thomas, he'd rather not have his son witness it, however.

As Dan reached them, he caught the nervous glimmer in Beth's gaze.

"Hi," Dan said. "Merry Christmas."

"Merry Christmas, Daniel," Granny said with a smile.

Dan held his hand out toward Rick, but Rick didn't return the gesture, and Dan dropped his hand to his side. He could see the point. This Christmas was a fresh start for Dan's business, but it was a heartbreaking goodbye for Rick's.

"I'm sorry, Mr. Thomas," Dan said quietly. "It's just business, though."

"Yep, I get that," Rick replied. "But don't ask me to celebrate with you."

"Okay then." Dan nodded. What else was he supposed to say? It wasn't like he could hand the store back over to the man. That old corner store might have been filled with memories, but from what he understood, it hadn't made a profit in years. Dan deserved a chance at a business of his own. Maybe his would be more profitable. He sure hoped so.

Rick didn't answer. He stalked away, leaving Dan alone with Granny and Beth. Dan watched him go, and his heart sank. He wouldn't want to undo his own good fortune, but he also didn't want to hurt Rick, either.

"Sorry," Beth murmured. "He's taken it pretty hard."

Ironic as it might seem to someone in Rick's position, Dan was hoping that he'd be able to give his own son a family business experience with that property. He wanted to work side by side with his boy, teaching him how to do a job well and how to take pride in something bigger than himself. Luke would earn his first dollar working for his dad, and one day maybe Dan would leave the tool shop to Luke so that he could use it to support his own family. Dan wanted that cozy, comfy picture of a family-run business—the very legacy that had just failed for the Thomases. But Rick's problem with him wasn't the store—it was Beth. Dan had promised her father that he'd do right by her, and he'd let her down. Rick had never liked Dan, and his buying the store wasn't going to change that.

"Beth is Rick's little girl," Granny said. "It's hard for a man to let his daughter go and get married. He's got to trust that the young man in question is going to do right by her."

Granny gave Dan a significant nod, and Dan glanced at Beth. She looked pained.

"Don't worry," Granny said. "I'll go have a talk with my son."

Dan watched as Granny went after Rick, her feet sure on the packed snow.

"I'm not sure how much that'll help," Dan said with a low laugh.

"Not much," Beth replied with a wry smile. "What a Christmas, Danny."

Her voice was dampened by sadness. Dan scanned for his son and saw that Luke had stopped to watch the kids getting their Santa pictures taken. He looked down at Beth. She was absently rubbing the top of her belly, her fair skin illuminated by the twinkle of pink lights on the tree behind them.

"Luke wants to see his mom," Dan said quietly.

"What?" Beth looked up at him. "Really?"

"And I know that it's normal, but—" Dan shook his head. "You know how complicated this one is."

"Does he remember her?" Beth asked.

"He says he doesn't." Dan sighed. "But there's an emotional memory. He knows he's missing something."

"His heart remembers her," Beth said.

"Lana isn't like you, Beth. You're thinking of your baby right now, but his mom hasn't checked up on him in five years."

"Does he blame you for that?" Beth asked.

"I hope not, but he might. I've told him that I'd let her visit…but how do I tell him that she doesn't want to?"

Luke had started to talk to a girl from his class—a girl he'd had a crush on for a couple of years now—and Dan smiled wistfully. This park—he wondered if it would occupy a special place in Luke's heart, too. An elementary-school crush didn't look like much from the adult side of things, but to a boy Luke's age it was huge. Luke would never admit to it, of course. But Emily R. came up in conversation about his school day an awful lot.

"Would you let Lana and Luke talk on the phone or something?" Beth asked.

Dan considered that for a moment. He could respect Lana, and he could wish her well, but he wouldn't play games when it came to Luke. He knew it was contradictory. He resented what Lana's abandonment had done to Luke, wanted her to be more of a mother to their son, but at the same time, he didn't trust her enough to let her in close.

"No," he said with a shake of his head. "I guess I don't trust her to walk away." He paused, listening to the sound of his own words as they echoed in his thoughts. "That sounds awful, doesn't it? I *want* her to abandon him again."

What kind of a man did that make him? He felt helpless right now. Luke was too young to think this through for himself. It was Dan's job to protect his son, but at what cost?

"You're scared," Beth replied. "You want her to respect boundaries, but you don't trust her to do that. That's not awful."

That summed it up rather well. He shot her a grateful glance. Maybe he wasn't as bad as he imagined. Dan watched Luke digging his boot into the snow as he and Emily R. talked.

"Yeah, I guess that's it," he agreed. "I need her to respect that Luke's with me now. But you know how much a parent loves a child, Beth... I don't think she could just walk away again. I know I couldn't once I'd had the chance to get to know my boy, and I'm afraid that she'd come back for him. In a more permanent way."

They were silent for a few moments, then Beth said, "I have no advice, Danny."

Dan's heart was heavy in his chest. "I asked Luke what he asked Santa for."

"What did he say?" Beth asked softly.

"He asked for his mom." He glanced down at her and saw tears welling in Beth's eyes.

"You have to do what's best for Luke, even if he thinks he knows better than you do."

But what *was* best for Luke? Would Dan look back on this and regret having caved to his own fear? Would Luke resent him? How could he even know?

A voiced boomed over the loudspeaker: "Let's all move toward the central tree, ladies and gentlemen! It's time to count down!"

Luke looked toward his father, and Dan beckoned him back over. The amplified voice started the countdown.

"Thirty…twenty-nine…twenty-eight…"

Luke arrived at Dan's side, and Dan put a hand on his son's shoulder. Regardless of what was out of their control, regardless of the things they wished for but couldn't have, it was Christmastime, and there were memories to be made.

"I always wondered why they started counting so high," Beth said with a low laugh. "They always did that."

"It's because it's more exciting that way," Luke said, leaning to look around Dan. "And because old people are slow."

"Don't call people old, Luke," Beth said with a small smile. "Your dad told me that it's rude. We both learned something."

"Oh, yeah." Luke blushed. "Fine. Elderly people are slow."

Dan shot Beth a grin—she'd backed him up, and that softened him more than anything else tonight. She turned toward the central tree. She was beautiful still...that hadn't changed. Beth Thomas had always been able to stop his heart.

"Fifteen, fourteen, thirteen, twelve..." People were counting along now, shouting out the numbers as Santa climbed the stage to the big theatrical button waiting for him.

"Does that really connect to the lights?" Luke asked dubiously.

"Yes," Dan said. "Of course."

Luke was growing up, and he was losing

faith in the fun things like Santa and big theatrical buttons. But the real world waiting for him wouldn't be better, or easier, or kinder. Dan was shielding his son from a lot of ugliness that Luke couldn't even imagine yet, but it was Dan's job to stand in the way as long as he could, and be a protective shadow. At least, he *thought* that was his job…

"Five, four, three—"

Dan glanced over at Beth just as she did the same and their eyes met. He didn't know what he was looking for—comfort, maybe? Just some understanding. All he'd ever wanted from Beth was for her to see things from his perspective for once, and maybe forgive him for being less than a superhero.

The big tree suddenly blazed into light, stripes of green and red light leading up to the top where a golden star shone like a beacon. The first strains of "O Christmas Tree" came out of the speakers, and the crowd oohed and aahed, then sang along.

"Zero…" Dan murmured.

O Christmas tree. O Christmas tree. Thy leaves are so unchanging…

There was truth in those words—Christmas froze this little crystal of hope in peo-

CHAPTER NINE

THE THOMAS FAMILY left the park shortly after
the Christmas tree was lit. Granny was tired
and cold, so Beth said goodbye to Danny and
Luke, then followed her father and grandmother back the way they'd come. As they
walked, irritation gnawed at Beth's peace
of mind.

Her father had wanted Beth to come along
for this tree-lighting ceremony for the sake
of family memories, but once they were
there, he'd snapped at Danny and marched
off. What good had that done? They all
lived in this town, and the Thomases' down-
ward financial spiral wasn't Danny's fault.
If anyone could be blamed, it was her father. He'd married someone without thinking things through and had let that new wife
call the shots at the business. Amazingly,
just after she left, the store went belly-up.
Granny seemed to believe that Linda was

ple's hearts despite all the reasons to give up. Life was hard and tiresome, but a Christmas tree represented something both fragile and unchanging: the hope people clung to for family and connection, for some love in this world.

What did any of them have without hope?

the reason the store had lasted as long as it had, but Beth wasn't convinced. At the very least, Linda had recognized that the store was worthless now and she'd ever so sweetly walked off with the solid cash.

And yet her father blamed Danny—the one person in this situation who had the least to do with the actual store.

"Dad, it isn't Danny's fault," Beth said as they came inside that evening. She stomped the snow off her boots and helped Granny get her things off.

"I know."

"So...you couldn't have shaken his hand?" Beth asked. "That was embarrassing. I know you're the tortured artist around here, but come on!"

"My issues with Daniel aren't financial," Rick said. "I've never liked that guy."

"Tonight was *your* idea, Dad."

Granny sighed and went the staircase, then looked back. "You two should stop fighting. It's not good for the baby."

Letting a lid off the frustration stewing would probably be beneficial to the baby. Beth was so tired of holding this in, mulling over it when she was alone, letting her words swirl fruitlessly inside her.

"Don't worry, Granny," Beth said. "Dad and I need to hash a few things out."

Granny muttered to herself and her footsteps creaked up the stairs as Beth turned back to her father.

"I had a good talk with Granny when she was lucid," she said, keeping her voice low. "Granny seems to think that Linda was the reason our store stayed afloat this long."

"I ran that store myself!" her father said irritably. He turned away and headed for the fridge.

"Granny says Linda gave a whole lot of advice. And you took it," Beth replied.

"So you think I followed bad advice and ended up losing the family business?" her father demanded, turning back. "So I'm the scatterbrained writer who has no idea about business?"

"That's exactly what I think. You're brilliant, Dad, but not where Linda was concerned."

"Because it's always Linda's fault, right?" her father quipped. "It's not like she disappeared, you know. She and I stay in contact, and the store going under had nothing to do with her."

Beth stared at him in disbelief. He'd been like a brick wall when it came to Linda, and even after filing for the divorce, he was still defending her?

"You're divorcing her!" Beth could almost scream in frustration. "Dad! She left you!"

"I'm well aware." That one had hurt him— she could hear it in the quiver of his voice. She didn't want to hurt him, but there were things that needed to be said.

"Then why are you defending her?" Beth shook her head. "She *is* the bad guy here. She walked off with all your investments so that you can't retire, left a business that she either knew couldn't last much longer or even sabotaged—"

"You're going too far with that one," her father said tiredly.

"Fine, I'll take back the sabotage, but, Dad, you're doing the same thing you've done for the last twenty years—you're siding with her."

Rick leaned against the counter and crossed his arms over his chest. It was the same look he'd give her every time she complained to him about Linda—tired, closed off.

"You didn't like her from the start," her father said.

"And yet you married her," Beth replied.

"I was supposed to stay single?" Her father shook his head. "What about my needs? I was lonely! I'd lost my wife, I had two kids to raise and I wanted some companionship, too."

"You could have chosen someone else," Beth shot back. "A better fit for the family!"

"I chose a good fit for *me*!" His voice nearly shook the kitchen. "That's how marriage works! She wasn't marrying the whole family—she was marrying me!"

"She was marrying *my dad*!" Why couldn't he see the problem? "I was a kid—I was part of that package!"

"Of course you were, but at the end of the day, you kids were going to grow up and move out—which you both did—and Linda and I would have our twilight years together. If I'd married someone you adored but who I wasn't as crazy about, where would that have left me? Marriage is about the couple. You chose that idiot Danny, and if he hadn't dumped the bombshell of some child from another relationship on you, you'd have married him regardless of *my* feelings!"

She would have, that was true. But not with kids in the picture.

"Linda hated me, Dad."

"She liked you fine." Rick shook his head.

"Liked me fine…that's what you're going with?" Beth's shook her head. "That was your goal for your daughter's life? You gave me a stepmother who *liked me fine*?"

"You weren't easy on her," he countered.

"I was *a kid*!" Beth rubbed her hands over her face. "I'd lost my mother, Dad. My mom who loved me more than life was dead, and my dad who was supposed to take over and be there for me found his comfort with a woman who was cold and distant. I was left to deal with it all alone!"

"Linda tried!" There was pleading in her father's voice. "You wouldn't let her close. You hated her because she wasn't your mom, and nothing she did was good enough."

No, Beth hadn't let Linda close, but she would have let her father in. He hadn't tried. He'd always sent Linda to talk to her instead. She'd wanted her father.

"I keep coming back to this…" Beth sank onto a kitchen chair. "You chose her, every time. When it came between me and Linda, you chose Linda."

"She was the adult, you were the child. It's what they say you're supposed to do in a blended family. The adults call the shots. So, yes, I backed Linda up." Rick sighed. "Beth, you're angry, and I get that. But I was doing my best for you. A twelve-year-old can't run her father's life."

The very advice she'd given to Danny— to do what he felt was best for Luke, regardless if Luke agreed. Because kids couldn't see the bigger picture, nor should they be expected to.

"A twelve-year-old shouldn't have been left in the care of an unloving woman," she said with a sigh. "Linda didn't like me, and she didn't hide it. She treated me like an unwanted problem. Then she cozied up to you. I don't know what she told you, but whatever it was, you believed her. Because I tried telling you over and over again that I was miserable, I was lonely, I felt misunderstood."

"I'm sorry," her father said quietly. "I thought—" He sighed. "I didn't realize."

"The thing is, Dad," Beth said quietly, "you didn't know because Linda wouldn't let you have any time alone with me."

Rick was silent for a moment, then he nodded slowly. "Okay, I see that one. I should have spent more time with you, just the two of us."

"But Linda didn't like it," she confirmed.

"She felt left out," Rick said. "We were supposed to be a family, and she wanted to be a part of things. I saw the softer side of Linda that she didn't show most people. She wanted to get along with you, kiddo. She really did."

Beth ran her fingers through her hair, pulling the errant strands away from her face. "I understand falling in love, Dad. I loved Danny with my whole heart, but I knew I couldn't be a stepmother. I *knew* that. I was willing to walk away because I couldn't be the stepmom his child needed."

"Your mom died." Her father's voice shook. "I couldn't stop that. I couldn't make her get better. And I tried so hard… When she died, I saw the hole that her death left in your heart, and I thought that if I gave you a stepmother, it could fix some of that pain."

"You were always enough, Dad."

They fell silent, and Beth met her father's gaze across the kitchen. She could see now that her father had tried, but he'd gotten it wrong. Just like Danny was trying, and maybe she was giving miserable advice because she couldn't see the whole picture, either. Everyone was just hoping for the best...

"How can I make it up to you?" her father asked at last.

"Just stop defending Linda."

Rick smiled sadly. "Okay."

Beth nodded, swallowed. She felt wrung out, and tears rose in her throat.

"Can I hug my little girl?" her father asked hopefully.

Beth pushed herself to her feet and crossed the room. Her father wrapped his arms around her. He pressed a kiss onto the top of her head just like he used to, and she let out a shaky sigh.

"I'm sorry," her father said again. "I'm so, so sorry."

Beth nodded against his shoulder, but she didn't have any words right now. Very soon, she'd have a daughter of her own, and that daughter wouldn't stay a baby. Beth could plan for success all she wanted, but that didn't mean Riley wouldn't have her own complaints one day.

But of one thing she was absolutely certain: the children needed to come first. It might be painful, and it might mean sacrifice, but Beth couldn't put up with anything less. Riley would always come first.

THE NEXT MORNING, Dan stood in the middle of the store and looked around. Luke had the day off school—a professional development day for the teachers. Luke had been planning on playing video games at home, but Dan had other plans for him. Today, Dan wanted his son to see the bones of the store they'd be running together.

That morning, Dan had come across a note Ralph had written to his wife, and Dan had texted Beth that he'd found something she might be interested in, but he hadn't spoiled the surprise. He had a feeling this might be one of the treasures she'd been hoping for— the piece of family history connected to her grandparents' love story. He was hoping that his own family could build just as much history in this exact spot, except he was doing this alone. The legacy that he was starting didn't include romance yet.

"What if I mess up?" Luke had been worrying about the pageant all morning.

"You won't. You know your lines," Dan said.

"But I might get nervous and forget them."

"Nah." Dan shook his head. "Not going to happen. Quit worrying, Luke. You know those lines."

Luke didn't look convinced. "What if I faint?"

Luke had suddenly realized at about ten o'clock last night that he'd be performing in front of half the town, and he'd started to panic a little bit. He'd been thinking up worst-case scenarios ever since.

Dan laughed. "Faint? Are you seriously worried about that?"

"It's possible!" Luke retorted.

Luke needed some distraction, and Dan knew exactly what to try—knocking apart shelves. Dan could do the job by himself a lot faster, but including Luke in the project was worth more to him right now.

"Aren't you curious what we're going to be doing today?" Dan asked.

Luke looked around. "What?"

"We're going to finish taking out the last of the shelves," Dan said. "Then we'll start getting ready to paint the walls."

"That's a lot of work." Luke didn't look quite so enthusiastic as Dan felt.

"Yeah, but think of how great it'll look once it's done," Dan replied. "Over there will be the counter for the cash register. We'll put in brand-new shelves, and that wall over there will be for displays of miter saws and drills and that sort of thing."

"Oh." Luke squinted.

"And I'll let you run the cash register," Dan added.

"You will?" He had the boy's interest now. "I could take the money and everything?"

"Sure! You just have to know how to count money. Can you do that?"

"I count my own money," Luke replied.

"That's a start," Dan said. "We'll practice so you're ready. But you'll be helping me to run this place, Luke. We'll be doing it together. I wanted to call the store Brockwood Tools because we're the Brockwood men."

"Can you call it Luke's Tools?" Luke asked.

"No." Danny laughed. "But nice try."

"If I help paint, will you pay me?" Luke asked.

"No," Danny said. "We're doing this because we're the Brockwood men, and this is our store. But when you start at the store after school, I'll start to pay you a bit."

"A real paycheck?" Luke's eyes lit up.

"That's right. You'll have earned it."

Luke nodded slowly, his gaze moving around the store with new energy. Dan could see the store materializing in Luke's mind's eye, and together, they'd make that vision a reality. It was a priceless lesson to teach a boy—how to turn an idea into a fact—and Dan was excited to be able to start this venture when Luke was old enough to glean some hands-on experience.

"So let's get this place cleaned up," Dan said. "What do you say?"

"Okay!" Luke looked around. "What do we do first?"

"Take this hammer," Dan said. "We're going to start knocking apart those old shelves. Then we'll take them outside."

That was the kind of job a kid could get

behind—demolition. Luke took the hammer and headed for the first shelf.

"Now, use your head," Dan said. "You want to hit the joints so that they'll break apart. Don't just smack stuff randomly, okay?"

"Yeah, I get it." Luke used tools with his dad all the time, so Dan wasn't too worried. It would be helpful and use up a bunch of eight-year-old energy at the same time… maybe even burn off some of that pageant anxiety. Dan called that a parenting win.

The door opened just as Luke made his first connection with the wood, and Beth startled. She was in her cream-colored winter coat, her belly peeking out the front. She brushed a blond tendril out of her face.

"Hi!" Dan said. "Sorry, we're just breaking apart some shelves."

"Oh…" She nodded. "Of course." Her gaze lingered on the hammer before she purposefully looked away. The pained look on her face dampened Dan's enthusiasm slightly. It was hard to plan your own future in the sight of someone else's heartbreak.

"I came across something I think you'll

want," Dan said, fishing the piece of paper out of his pocket and handing it over.

Beth opened the crinkling page and scanned the contents. She looked up, amazed.

"Right?" Dan said.

"Where did you find this?" she asked.

Ralph had made a list of supplies for the store years ago, and at the end was a heart-felt note.

Smart and beautiful—I'm one lucky man. I'd marry you all over again, Elinor. Happy anniversary. Tonight, I cook. Ralph

"It was in the desk in the back room," Dan said. "I thought Granny might want it."

"I'm sure she will!" Beth shook her head. "Thank you for this."

Luke took up a pounding rhythm, and Dan gestured with his chin toward the outside door. Beth took his hint and they stepped outside. It was colder on the porch, but at least the noise wasn't quite so rattling. Dan grabbed his coat on his way outside and put it on but didn't bother doing up the zipper.

Beth shrugged her coat up higher around her ears.

"He's having fun," Beth said with a small smile. Dan glanced back toward the store.

"Yeah, he's pretty excited. I'm trying to get him to see what we can build together." Dan felt his smile slip. "I know this is insensitive of me. I'm trying to get my son excited about the very thing you grew up with."

"And why shouldn't you?" Beth replied. "It was great. I used to come down here after school and my dad would let me sit on the stool behind the counter and talk to people. He'd sit in the back room with his computer and get stuck into whatever chapter he was working on."

Her empathy was a relief. She seemed to have gotten better at that over the last five years.

"I loved it," she went on. "My brother and I hated doing the real work—putting out the latest newspapers and getting the crates ready for milk delivery…that kind of thing. But it was good for us. We learned how to do a job right the first time."

Beth turned around, looking at the faded sign overhead that read North Fork Corner

Store. A few snowflakes swirled in the air, spinning past them like fluffy parachutes.

"I'm hoping Luke will have some memories like yours," Dan said, clearing his throat. "It's a really great way to grow up—contributing to something. Knowing you belong."

"Until you don't."

Dan heard the reproach in those words. Maybe that empathy was in shorter supply than he thought.

"I'd be stupid to pass up a chance like this, Beth."

"I know…" She shook her head. "I'm not talking about the store. I'm talking about this town. I didn't think that five years away would change so much. Or maybe it isn't North Fork. Maybe it's me. I don't fit here the same way."

Her blue gaze met his, and her breath hung in the air in front of her, a snowflake clinging to one strand of hair. Why did she have to be so beautiful still? It wasn't fair.

"Give it time," he said. "You'll settle back in."

"Maybe," Beth agreed. "I had a good talk with Dad about Linda."

"Oh?" Dan eyed her curiously. That conversation had been a long time coming.

"He admitted that Linda stopped him from spending time alone with me," she said. "He said she felt left out if she wasn't in the middle of everything."

"And he acknowledged that?" Dan asked dubiously. Rick had always been rather blind to Linda's shortcomings.

"Finally." She sucked in a deep breath. "It's something."

"It must have felt good to talk that through," he said.

She tilted her head to one side. "Yes and no. Things had to be said, but it's too late to fix anything."

The wind picked up and flipped the corner of Beth's coat so that the side of her shirt-clad stomach was exposed. She shivered, and Dan stepped closer. He tugged her coat straight again. He should have stepped back, but he couldn't quite bring himself to do it—not when he stood so near to her that he could feel the warmth of her belly against his taut stomach. So he held on to the sides of her jacket against the wind's gusts and tugged her closer still.

There had been a time when standing together against the elements was natural, but now it felt forbidden. He'd kissed her before, and he'd said he'd control himself. She wasn't his to shelter anymore, even though he had a hard time curbing that instinct with her. He'd darn well have to.

"Thank you..." She shivered again, but she didn't pull away.

"Better?" he murmured.

She nodded, then smiled ruefully. "I'm regretting not investing in that maternity jacket now."

"I'll bet." Funny—he liked sharing these pregnancy problems with Beth. He'd missed this before Luke was born, and being here for Beth almost seemed to be a second chance. *Except this isn't my baby, and she isn't my girlfriend, either...*

"Beth," he said softly. "Are *you* okay?"

"More or less." Those dark blue eyes met his again, and he had to hold himself back from reaching out and touching her.

"If you ever need anything," he said, "I'm here for you. And I mean that. Anything."

He reached up to brush a snowflake from her hair, and he caught her gaze—the big blue eyes that had always been able to capture him. He could see both the vulnerability and the sweetness that had always been there.

He wished he could pull her closer, block out the last of that cold wind and do what he'd always done before—lower his lips over hers and kiss her so thoroughly that he left her weak in the knees.

Her lips parted as if she were about to say something, and Dan swallowed with the effort of *not* kissing her.

It was only then that he noticed that the hammering inside had stopped, and the door suddenly flung open. Dan took an instinctive step away from Beth and the cold flooded around him once more.

"Hey, Beth?" Luke began, then he stopped short. "What's going on?"

"Nothing, son," Dan said, clearing his throat. "We were just talking. What do you need?"

"I wanted to ask Beth what happens if I forget my lines at the pageant," Luke said.

"Um…" Beth licked her lips and looked slightly flustered. Dan couldn't help the grin that warmed his face. So she'd been caught up in that moment, too. At least he wasn't the only one.

"Are you going to be there to see it?" Luke pressed.

"Of course," Beth said. "And I'll tell you what—I'll sit in the front row and remind you of your lines if you forget."

"You will?" Luke asked, relief flooding his features. That was all it took? Why hadn't Dan thought of that?

"If your dad doesn't mind," Beth added hastily.

He was to blame for this one anyway. Neither of them were thinking straight, but even so, she'd just done the impossible and calmed Luke's stage fright. How could he refuse her?

"Yeah, of course," Dan said. "It'll be fine, Luke. See? I told you."

Luke disappeared inside, and the sound of hammering started up again. Dan heaved a sigh. If his son hadn't clattered out when he had… No, he'd already made a fool of himself once.

"I should get back," Beth said, taking another step away from him. He wished she'd stay for a few more minutes, but it was better that she left. He knew what he wanted with her, and he needed a few minutes alone to quell those urges.

"Okay," he said.

"I'll see you."

Dan nodded and lifted his hand in a wave. She headed toward the street, her steps careful and steady. The snowfall began to thicken, and he watched her go for another few seconds before he turned back toward the store.

New starts—that was what this was all about, wasn't it? He wasn't supposed to go back to old habits, especially when those habits couldn't be good for Luke. His son had to be the priority—there was no question. If only his emotions would catch up with his reason.

CHAPTER TEN

BETH'S HEART FLUTTERED in her chest as she walked the three blocks home. There had been something between them in that moment when Danny caught her eye—a charged connection that was nothing like the sizzle they'd shared five years ago. This was different…deeper, less demanding, but most definitely there.

Would he have kissed her again had Luke not interrupted them? They'd already done this once, and they'd both acknowledged that it wasn't going to work. She couldn't be the woman he wanted, and she couldn't trust him. Yet, despite all those excellent reasons to keep their distance, they'd still been caught in a moment when she'd expected him to kiss her again. The question was, would she have allowed him?

"Of course not," she said aloud. She and Danny were very clear on where things stood. Nothing had changed, except they were obviously still attracted to each other. Which was normal, wasn't it?

She was trying to make this logical, because she needed it to be logical. She had a baby on the way, a heartbroken father, a grandmother with dementia… It was all she could handle right now, and her conflicting feelings for Danny were just too much. The baby shifted in her belly, and she sighed. She had her priorities right here—her daughter.

When Beth got home, she found Granny asleep in her chair in the living room, an infomercial playing on TV. Beth got herself a bowl of soup and a sandwich, and after she had finished eating and cleaning up, there was a knock on the front door. Beth went back into the living room—Granny didn't even stir; her soft snoring continued. Beth tugged her sweater closer around her and answered the door.

Linda stood on the step, her straightened, ash-blond hair ruffling in the winter wind. She wore a green parka and white leather gloves, and while this house used to be her home, she no longer belonged here. She looked foreign. Uncomfortable. Beth had to curb the urge to simply slam the door shut again.

This was supposed to be over, but there she stood—Linda, in the flesh.

"Hello," Beth said curtly.

"My goodness…look at you." Linda smiled tentatively. "Your dad told me about the baby, of course, but… Hello, Beth."

It was the exact response that Beth expected from her image-concerned ex-stepmother. Linda was an expert on proprieties, including when babies should be entering the scene. Beth had landed on the wrong side of decency—at least in Linda's view.

"Yes, definitely pregnant," Beth said with a cool smile. "You dodged out in time. No reflection on you at all."

Linda's smile slipped. "I suppose congratulations are in order."

"Thank you." Beth knew the proper responses just as well as her stepmother did, and they could do this all day. But it was cold, and Beth tugged her sweater a bit closer.

"Uh—is your father around?" Linda asked.

"No, he's out." Job hunting, most likely,

but Beth wouldn't tell her that. Let her assume that Rick had a new lineup of eligible women after him. That would serve Linda right. Except Beth was supposed to be glad that Linda was out of the picture, so she knew that this desire to see Linda wounded wasn't right or defensible.

"Could I come in?" Linda asked.

Beth sighed and stepped back. "Sure. Granny's asleep, so…"

"Oh…" Linda lowered her voice and went in. Linda seemed bigger inside the house, somehow, like she'd gained power by crossing the threshold.

"Come through to the kitchen," Beth said, and Linda followed her. Once in the kitchen, she pulled out the chair she'd always sat in at the kitchen table, then took off her jacket. There was something too familiar in the way Linda moved about the house. It was understandable, of course—Linda had lived here for twenty years—but still, it rankled Beth.

"So how are you doing?" Linda asked.

"Fine." Beth nodded slowly. "And you?"

"Not great," Linda said. "This divorce has been difficult."

Beth hadn't expected that level of honesty, and she eyed Linda warily. Why were they doing this? Why was Linda even here? If she'd come for sympathy over her failed marriage, she'd definitely come to the wrong place. There was a beat or two of silence.

"Your dad is really excited about your baby," Linda offered.

"You and Dad keep up, do you?" Beth asked woodenly. Her father had told her as much, but Beth was feeling difficult.

"We talk." Linda nodded. "He's looking forward to being a grandfather."

That was more than her father had said to her on the subject. So far, her dad had worried about money, tried to convince her to get child support and suggested she put her feet up. But any kind of excitement about his granddaughter had never been evident.

"Linda, why are you here?" Beth asked at last.

"Well, two reasons, actually," Linda replied. "I have something to give to your father, and I thought it was only proper to do it in person. And I have a baby gift for you."

Only proper—that had been Linda to the bone. Everything she did followed proper etiquette, and she'd required the same formal perfection from Beth. Beth used to drive her stepmother crazy by flouting the rules, but she'd learned as much as she'd scorned.

Linda reached into her purse and pulled out two envelopes. One, the smaller of the two, she passed to Beth.

"It's a gift card," Linda said. "I hope that's all right. I didn't know what you needed, and I thought it would come in handy. I chose a gender-neutral card since ultrasounds can be wrong."

"Thank you," Beth said. She didn't open it, and she nodded toward the other envelope. "I hope you aren't taking my father to court. You've already cleaned him out."

Linda's face colored. "No, I'm not. I'm returning half the investments."

"You're—" Beth stared at Linda in shock. "Really?"

"Yes. It only seemed—" Linda didn't finish.

Proper. Of course. Beth had heard that over and over again, but mostly it had seemed like an excuse to be hard on people. The strict expectations of everyone, in every circumstance. This time, it had seemed to come from a different place inside Linda, a softer place.

"That's very decent of you," Beth said. "Thank you. He needs it."

"Well…" Linda licked her lips. "I'm not the complete ogre you think I am."

Beth sighed. "Do you want some tea while you wait?"

If Linda had come with a peace offering like that, then perhaps she could be offered some small refreshment.

"Thank you, I would." Linda smoothed her gloves on her lap. "If it isn't too much bother."

Beth raised one eyebrow, then flicked the switch on the electric kettle. Then she took a seat opposite Linda.

"Do you mind if I ask you something?" Beth asked.

"Sure." Linda's expression seemed a little wary, perhaps expecting a clever trap.

"Why did you marry my dad?" Beth asked.

Linda blinked, dropped her gaze to her lap, then looked up with tears misting her eyes. "I loved him."

"Was it his career?" she pressed. "You always were one of his biggest fans."

"I loved his writing," Linda replied, "but I loved him more. I encouraged him to write because he was so good at it, and because it fulfilled him. I never wanted to come between him and his passion."

Apparently, she didn't mind coming between him and his daughter, though.

"But Michael and I were also in the picture," Beth pressed, not overcome with sympathy. "Two kids, my dad had lost the love of his life… Why take that on?"

Linda pursed her lips. "I thought I could do it. Apparently, I was wrong."

"Do *what*, though?" Beth asked, because she was honestly curious. Why had Linda even bothered with a man who had two kids if she wasn't the nurturing sort?

"I thought that I had something to offer," Linda said slowly. "I might not have been your mother, but I did have life experience and knowledge that might benefit a child. I thought that if your father and I loved each other enough, it might make up for other things."

Other things... "You didn't think you should love his children, too?"

"But I did." Linda didn't even blink.

"You loved me?" Beth asked incredulously.

"I tried to." Linda shrugged faintly. "And I did. I suppose it depends on your definition of love. If you're asking if I felt warm and fuzzy feelings toward you, well, no. You hated me too much for that. But I did everything else. I drove you to friends' homes, I taught you manners and tried to point out clothes that would look good on you. And I stayed. No matter how much you hated me, I *stayed*."

She had indeed stayed—her presence had been like concrete in Beth's life. Linda hadn't budged for anything. Until now.

"It wasn't enough, though," Beth said. "I needed someone who could feel something warm and fuzzy for me."

"Nothing would have been enough," Linda replied with a shake of her head. "I wasn't your mother. Simple as that. Your father thought that me being a woman would give you something important, especially at your vulnerable age. You were on the cusp of womanhood without anyone to show you the way."

"There is one more thing I've been wondering about lately," Beth said slowly. "I want to know why you hated letting me be alone with my own father."

Linda was silent for a moment. She picked up her gloves, then smoothed them over her knee again. She seemed to be ordering her thoughts—or evading. Beth wasn't sure which. But then Linda said, "You were sixteen when you asked your father to take you and your brother out for dinner without me. You asked him upstairs in the hallway." She glanced toward the staircase. "You thought I was asleep, and you told him that all you wanted was to have it like it used to be for one evening. As a gift to you. A night without me."

That hadn't been quite the sentiment...or maybe it was.

"I needed time with my dad," Beth replied. "I never had that. You were always there."

"I was his wife!" Something close to anger sparked in Linda's gaze. "This was my home, too! This was all I had! In my own home,

I was hated by my husband's daughter. At least Michael gave me a chance. So it wasn't easy for me, either."

"If you'd just given me some space…" Beth heaved a sigh. "I know I was difficult, Linda. And I apologize for that. I was really angry that my mother had died, and I didn't know how to process that. Then Dad fell in love with you, and that felt like a betrayal to my mom."

"I get it." Linda nodded. "I always told you I didn't expect to replace her."

"I thought that meant that you couldn't love me like she had."

"And I couldn't." Linda shook her head. "Let's just be honest. I *wasn't* your mom. I never had children of my own, but I had a mother, and I do understand that love. I could have loved you in my own way…if you'd let me."

It was too little, too late, though. Beth's formative years were behind her. Perhaps Linda had learned a few of these lessons in the process, too. They'd been through the worst of it, and Beth couldn't help but wonder if there hadn't been some salvageable memories under all that ugliness.

"If you could do it again," Beth said. "Would you still have married him?"

"And end up heartbroken?" Linda's eyes misted again. "No."

That's what Beth had thought. Linda had done her best, it would seem, but it hadn't been enough for a grief-stricken twelve-year-old girl. Manners and etiquette wouldn't fill that hole left by her mother's passing. And watching her father love a woman who'd never fully love her—that had only made it worse. Perhaps Linda hadn't been the devil, after all, but it still hadn't worked.

"So what happened?" Beth asked. "Why didn't it work between you and Dad after Michael and I were gone?"

"Because of that store." Linda sighed and shook her head. "He always loved that store more than he loved me. I was there to support him and help him create his next great novel, but he relied on that rickety corner store to inspire him…not me. He treated it more like a good-luck charm than an actual business. And when I told him it would fail, he resented me for it. But it did fail—because its time had passed. Holding on to that relic of family history wouldn't make it financially viable."

Linda never had been much of a sentimentalist. Her father had loved that store more than he'd loved Linda, but not more than his kids. And Linda had been threatened by her husband's love for his children. She'd held on to Rick with a vise grip and refused to leave his side for a moment. In case of…what? In case he bonded with his daughter without her? But the store had somehow become the final straw.

"It was the family store." Beth shook her head. "Of course it mattered to him."

"I didn't say it wasn't important," Linda said simply. "I just said it couldn't continue. And we fought about it constantly until we got tired of the fighting."

Beth heard her father's footsteps on the porch outside, which Linda seemed to hear at the same time, because she sucked in a breath and held it. Beth stood and got down a couple of mugs. She'd promised tea, after all.

When the back door opened, Rick came inside, but he didn't seem surprised by their visitor.

"Linda," he said quietly. "I saw your car out front."

"Hello, Ricky."

Ricky. Linda had always called him that, and it had always irritated Beth as a girl, but now she could hear the longing. Linda missed him.

"I was just starting tea, Dad," Beth said. "But maybe you could finish that. I'll let you two talk."

Her father gave her a grateful nod, and Beth headed toward the door that led to the living room. Granny was still napping, and Beth crept past and headed up the staircase, the old boards creaking underfoot.

She'd never seen her father or her stepmother as adults with romantic needs, but perhaps it was time to grow up. Resentful of Linda or not, Beth knew what she'd seen in there, and it was heartbreak. Her father wasn't the only one struggling. Linda was, too. Letting go of a man she had loved dearly—even if it was the right thing to do—hurt desperately. For that, Linda had Beth's sympathy.

Luke wandered around the house getting ready to go. Getting an eight-year-old kid out of the house took time. At the moment, Luke was barefoot, and he sang his lines over and over again until he started to get the words wrong.

"Give it a break, buddy," Dan said. "You're going to be fine. You'll see! Just imagine people in their underwear."

"Dad, that's just embarrassing." Luke shot his father an annoyed look. "And kind of inappropriate."

Dan chuckled. "Luke, you're going to be fine. I'll be in the front row."

"Beth, too, right?"

That stabbed just a little. If only Luke knew how badly Dan had wanted Beth to be a part of all this five years ago. But she'd left. This Christmas pageant tradition was *theirs*. It didn't include Beth.

"Why does it matter if Beth is there?" Dan asked. "I'll be there. You'll be fine!"

"I don't know. I like her. And she knows my lines."

"*I* know your lines." Dan was feeling a little defensive. "And I'll be in the front. Sing to me. That'll make it less stressful, right? Sing it like you're just practicing in the kitchen." Dan paused, giving his son a once-over. "Where are your socks?"

"I don't have them yet."

"Ticktock." Dan tapped his watch. "And brush your teeth—really well this time!"

Beth *would* be there…he wasn't sure how he felt about that. He'd seen the way Luke looked at Beth, the way the boy softened around her. It wasn't that Dan couldn't sympathize, because he found himself reacting in the same ways, except Dan knew the score here, and Luke didn't. Luke wanted a mother—Dan knew that well enough—but *not her…* If Luke had latched on to any other woman, Dan could have felt good about it, but Beth? Maybe Luke was more like him than he thought—maybe they were like two moths to the same flame.

Parenting was never-ending. There were no breaks, no time off, no clocking out. The rewards, however, were that much deeper. Like when he taught Luke how to skate, and the gleam of pride that shone in his son's eyes…or these pageants, where Luke was always so excited to be onstage. Until this year, at least. Now, Luke was a nervous wreck, and instead of turning to Dan for reassurance, he was turning to Beth.

"Come on, Luke! Let's go!"

Luke emerged from the bathroom. "Dad?"

"Yeah?"

"Do you think Mom would want to see me as Townsperson Number Four?"

Dan ran a hand through his hair, trying to calm his simmering irritation. Tonight—just for tonight—couldn't Dan be enough?

"I don't know, buddy," Dan replied truthfully. "But I sure do. Come on. Let's not be late."

Half an hour later at town hall, Dan gave Luke a squeeze goodbye, and the boy dashed off behind the stage to get ready with the rest of the cast. Dan made his way through the auditorium filled with folding chairs. They'd just made it, and the auditorium was already filling up. He paused and scanned the rows, spotting Beth in the very front. Her blond hair fell in glossy waves around her shoulders. She wore a pale blue sweater that brought out the color of her eyes, and when she turned toward him, his breath caught. He had to stop reacting like this…

"Hi," Dan said as she pulled her jacket off the seat she'd saved for him. "Did you have to fight to save this seat?" There were jackets laid across other seats next to him.

"Just about." She smiled back. "But no one wants to argue too much with a pregnant lady. I used my advantage."

Dan could make out the scent of her perfume—something soft and fruity—as he sank down next to her. He pulled his attention away from those details. He was here as a dad, not as company for Beth. The curtains were pulled over the stage, but he could hear rustling behind it.

"Luke's pretty nervous," he said. He'd keep himself on point here.

"Still?" Her voice was soft. "Poor guy. The stage can be pretty intimidating, I guess."

"I guess." Except Luke had never seemed to mind it before. Maybe this was just part of getting older—realizing that embarrassment was a possibility.

"You must be proud of him," Beth added.

"Yeah, for sure." Dan nodded, facing the closed curtain.

"Danny?"

He glanced over at her, then sighed. "Yeah?"

"What?" She shook her head at him—the same way she used to years ago when he was mulling over something he wasn't ready to talk about.

"Nothing." He swallowed, then lowered his voice more. But holding out on her had never been good for them. Maybe it was time to let the last of those old habits drop. "Fine, I'm…frustrated with myself. I don't think I kept things appropriate yesterday at the store."

"Oh…" She nodded. "Well—I was thinking about that, too. Maybe it's time to stop beating ourselves up and accept that we have chemistry, Danny."

"That's not useful if we're wanting to keep this platonic." He shot her a wry smile.

"Sure it is." She gave him only the slightest smile in return. "We always were attracted to each other. It's on a chemical level. It stands to reason that we'd still feel some—" She shrugged.

"Attraction?" he concluded.

Color tinged her cheeks. "It's reasonable."

That kiss needed to stay a onetime thing. They couldn't fall back into a broken relationship.

"And what are we supposed to do about it?" he asked. Because from where he was sitting, that wasn't going away, which bothered him.

"I think admitting it is half the battle," she replied. "I mean, putting it out there—knowing that we have a physical attraction—"

"You said chemical," he said quietly.

"Stop teasing." She was utterly serious. "At least for me, it helps. I mean, the mystery is the appealing part, isn't it? Well, we've done all of this before, and we know how it ends. If we can just admit to the attraction, I think we can dampen it."

Maybe she had a point. It was harder to cross those lines when both of them knew what was happening.

"You're wiser than I thought," he said grudgingly.

They fell silent, and Dan turned his attention back to that closed curtain.

"Luke wanted you here, especially," Dan admitted after a moment. It still stung a little to say. But if they were going to be open, maybe it could include this.

"It's the baby," she said softly.

"What?" He glanced back at her.

She rubbed a hand over her belly. "All the kids are the same. They're drawn to pregnant women and babies. There's one mom who keeps trying to get some privacy to feed her infant, and the kids keep on interrupting her. And Luke first started talking to me because he was curious about the baby coming. It's natural, I think."

Was it only that—a child's curiosity? Luke had been asking about his mother lately, too, so maybe that was it. Maybe Beth's pregnancy had been drawing Luke in, not Beth herself.

"Be careful with him, Beth," Dan said seriously.

"What do you mean?" Beth leaned closer, her gaze locked on his face.

"He's a fragile kid," Dan said. "Don't promise him anything you can't deliver. He's had enough broken promises in his life."

"You mean his mom," she clarified.

Yes, Lana. But Dan couldn't forget that Beth had rejected Luke, too, right at the beginning. Beth had looked down at Luke's sleeping face and decided against being with them. For all her judgment of Lana, she'd been able to walk away, too.

"Just be careful," Dan repeated.

She nodded, then leaned back in her seat.

After a moment, she said, "Linda's back in town. She dropped by yesterday to see my dad."

Dan looked over at her in surprise, his worry shrinking in the background to his curiosity. "How'd that go?"

"She and Dad talked for a while. She left." Beth sighed. "It's not my business… I know that. But this won't be easy on Dad. He needs to heal."

This would be Rick's first Christmas single, and Dan knew how hard that was. The Christmas after his breakup with Beth had been misery. Every happy Christmas sight and smell brought back memories that tore his heart open all over again. It would be the same for Rick, no doubt.

"Did you talk to Linda at all?" Dan asked.

Beth nodded. "A little bit."

"How's she doing?" he asked. Everyone had missed Linda around town. She'd moved away when she and Rick split up, but she'd been a part of things for two decades.

"She misses him." Sympathy swam in her blue eyes. He hadn't expected that reaction from her, but he didn't have the chance to ask anything else because the band started to tune up, and for a couple of minutes any conversation was drowned out by instruments.

Dan was used to doing this alone—waiting for Luke's appearance. Somehow it felt like if a dad smiled big enough and clapped hard enough, he could carry his kid through anything. This year, while he was conflicted about Luke's growing friendship with Beth, Dan had to admit that it was nice to have someone else watching for Luke. Another person to carry Luke through it. If Beth had married him, this could have been their life together. What was it that she'd said? *Danny, asking me to marry you and asking me to be a stepmother to your child are two different proposals...* But now she was enjoying the son *he'd* raised. Whether they were attracted to each other or not, that wasn't fair.

The lights lowered, and Dan settled back as the curtains opened and the MC came out to welcome everyone to this year's Christmas pageant. In years past, Dan had watched other people's kids on the stage, and he'd wondered if they'd known how lucky they were. They had families in the audience, a community that enjoyed their limited acting skills, and the safety of this small town in northern Alberta where not only did everyone know everyone, but they were all taken care of. Dan had wanted to give Luke all those happy childhood memories he'd never had as a kid.

Except Dan realized that it felt nice to have a woman next to him. He just wasn't sure that he wanted to share this with Beth. She was the one who'd thought she was too good for this package.

The stage was set, a couple of teens came out in costume and the story began. To the side, the kids portraying townspeople were walking around, looking in shop windows. Except for Townsperson Number Four. Luke stood there frozen, his lips white. Dan sat up straighter, and Luke looked toward his dad, his eyes wide with panic.

And Dan's heart sank.

CHAPTER ELEVEN

THE AUDITORIUM WAS WARM, and Beth fanned herself with the program. She'd seen how hard everyone had worked on this play, and it was nice to be seeing the fruition of all that effort. The baby wriggled inside her, and she rubbed a hand over her stomach. Beth glanced at Danny, but his eyes were locked on his son. As she turned her attention to Luke, he looked pale and scared. But given a few minutes, he'd be bound to relax, wouldn't he?

The townspeople were only supposed to be milling about right now anyway. Beth had already seen the whole play. Luke scanned the front row, and when he saw his father, he gave a pained smile. Then Luke turned those saucer eyes on Beth.

She gave him her most enthusiastic smile and a thumbs-up. Luke's shoulders relaxed slightly, and he licked his lips.

The little girl next to him lifted the microphone and sang her lines, then she handed the mic over to Luke. Luke opened his mouth, but nothing came out. He swallowed, tried again, but still nothing. There was an awkward silence, then the girl next to him took the mic back and the play continued…

Luke's expression crumpled, and his chin quivered. Tears welled in his eyes, but they didn't fall. His two lines. He'd been proud of those lines, she knew, and he'd missed them. The play had rolled on without his contribution.

Beth looked at Danny, and he glanced down at her, his son's anguish mirrored in his own eyes.

"Is he going to be okay?" Beth whispered.

"I think so…" Danny winced. "Oh, man."

Yes, that summed it up. Somehow, she'd thought that Luke's nerves would evaporate when he finally faced the moment, but apparently not. She was struck by Danny's reaction, though—he was taking this just as hard as Luke was, if not harder.

"It's just one mistake," Beth whispered. "It's no big deal!"

"Of course it's not," Danny agreed. "But

he's going to feel differently about that. You don't know Luke."

Was there reproach in those words? It was true that she didn't know Luke, but that didn't mean she was wrong, either. It was one mistake, and no one would even remember it. Luke's role in the play was as a townsperson, and he'd been on the stage most of the play. His role mattered, even without those lines.

They sat there for the rest of the play, watching Luke move with the townspeople, his shoulders stooped. When the actors took their bow at the end of the play, Beth clapped a little louder for the last row of townspeople. As they exited and the lights came up, Beth leaned toward Danny.

"He did a great job!" she whispered. "If you make it seem like a big deal, then he'll feel like it was. Just...relax."

"Parenting advice?" Danny raised his eyebrows, and Beth felt heat bloom in her cheeks. Would he throw this in her face forever now?

"Danny, I can have some good ideas without having an eight-year-old of my own."

Gone were the days when she was the one with all the answers, and it was more humbling still that Danny seemed to be ever so aware of that. Why even bring her along? If she was just one of those childless people full of useless advice—

Danny stood and gathered up his coat. "Sorry. I'm worried about Luke. That's all."

Beth could see that. He wasn't the same old Danny—he was a dad first and foremost. She didn't belong here with him and Luke. She wasn't part of their family, their bond. Luke was now the one closest to Danny's heart— as it should be. But it felt strange being on the outside when she was used to being so much closer to this man. Maybe being here tonight had been a mistake. She should have sensed that she was overstepping and backed out before this.

"I should probably head home," she said, rising to her feet. "Luke will need you right now—" She bent to grab her jacket and scarf.

"Actually…" Danny's tone softened. "If you could tell him that he did a great job, and…not act like his missed lines were a big deal…he'll believe you."

She smiled tentatively. "You sure?"

"Yeah. I'm his dad. He knows I have to support him no matter what. As much as I hate it, hearing it from you might actually make a difference."

"I feel like this is a dad-son thing…" she said.

"Let me put it this way," Danny said, his tone low. "I wish it were a dad-son thing, but he's growing up, and his world is a whole lot bigger than my opinion. So I guess I need to let other people be an influence, too."

"Oh…" She could tell by the look on his face that those words hadn't been easy to say.

"And he likes you. Guess we Brockwood guys share the same Achilles' heel." He had the same teasing glint in his eye she'd always loved.

Beth smiled wanly. "A genetic predisposition to blonde know-it-alls?"

"What can I say?" His dark eyes met hers. "Stick around?"

"Okay." When he asked like that…

Beth watched as Danny headed around the side of the stage and disappeared. She stood there for a moment, her hand on her belly as the baby hiccuped inside her. Danny still seemed to feel something for her—more than simple physical attraction—and as much as she hated to admit to it, he wasn't the only one. He was older now, a little more stubborn and definitely less willing to be bent to her will, but Danny would always be the guy she almost married. There was no erasing that.

She rubbed a small circle on the top of her belly. The baby hiccuped again, and she laughed softly.

"Hold your breath," she whispered. Or was the advice to drink a glass of water? Soon enough she'd have to brush up on her parental advice. And maybe Danny could help her out...seeing as he'd have been down this path before her.

Beth chatted with some of the people she knew. Everyone asked the same questions: When was the baby due? How was she feeling? Did she know if it was a boy or a girl? The one thing they very politely avoided was the question of the father. That news had probably spread.

A few minutes later, as she was saying goodbye to some old neighbors, she heard the clunk of boots behind her and turned to see Danny and Luke headed in her direction.

Luke looked dejected, and he walked half a step ahead of his dad, his winter coat unzipped and his mittens and hat held in his arms in front of him. She met Danny's gaze, and he reached forward and ruffled Luke's hair.

"Hi, Luke!" Beth grinned at him. "You did great! Nice job!"

"Hey." Luke dropped his hat and mittens onto the chair next to her, and then sank down into a different seat.

"You were a great Townsperson Number Four," Dan said. "And the play was great, too."

"I forgot my lines, Dad!" Luke didn't look like he was in the mood to be cajoled.

"Your part wasn't just about those two lines," Beth said. "Your part was very important. They needed a strong actor to be a believable townsperson, and you did that!"

"I forgot my lines!" Tears welled up in Luke's eyes. "And I practiced so hard, too…"

"That's the thing with live productions," Beth said. "On TV, they can do lots of takes. Actors forget their lines all the time and they just redo it. But onstage, there are no redos, so sometimes, there are mistakes. But that doesn't ruin it. It's just part of a live performance. A professional carries on anyway— just like you did."

"You think?" Luke looked up dubiously.

"I know." She gave him a decisive nod. "For a fact."

"Hey, it could have been worse," Danny said. "When I had a part in the Christmas play, I messed up, too. I was supposed to rev the engine and drive the motorcycle across the stage, but I hit the gas too hard and drove it right off the stage."

A smile tickled the corners of Luke's mouth. "What happened?"

"Luckily, I didn't hit anyone," he replied. "But I was really embarrassed. I was an adult at the time, too. Turned out that was the best part of the play for people. It even made it into the local newspaper. I was a star."

Beth grinned. Poor Danny had been introverted, and all the attention had been agonizing for him. She'd felt awful having begged him to participate that year. It was that same Christmas that he'd proposed at the tree-lighting ceremony... Alone. Away from everyone. She felt a wave of sadness at the memory, and her smile slipped.

"So it could have been worse, son," Danny said. "A couple of lines is nothing."

"Nothing at all," Beth agreed.

"Huh…" Luke shrugged. "Okay. I guess."

"You need to celebrate, Luke," Beth said. "Actors go out and celebrate their success, and your play was wonderful. I think a treat is in order."

"Yeah?" Luke looked up at his father.

"I have a big bucket of chocolate ice cream at home," Danny said. "And a jar of chocolate sauce. I'm pretty sure there are marshmallows in the cupboard somewhere…"

"Okay!" Luke grinned. "Are you coming, too, Beth?"

"Oh, I'd better not…" Beth shot an apologetic look at Danny. He wouldn't want her there, she was sure. It was time for her to bow out and let Danny take over with his son.

"How come?" Luke turned to his father. "We can invite her, right, Dad?"

"Uh…" Danny glanced from Luke to Beth. "It is a whole bucket of ice cream, after all. You'd be doing me a favor by eating some of it."

"Please?" Luke turned big brown eyes up at her. This kid had the whole puppy-dog look nailed down. But wouldn't she be intruding?

"Beth." Danny's voice was low and warm.

She looked up, and he shot her a slow smile. "You want to come by for ice cream?"

In that moment, he could have been the old Danny again, and she could have been the old Beth, slim and lithe, so in control... Except both of them had changed more than they liked to admit.

"Okay," she agreed.

"Good."

Beth started to put on her coat, and Danny held it for her as she got her other arm into the sleeve. Pregnancy had made so many things difficult lately. Luke wrapped his scarf around his neck, then struggled with his zipper.

"You sure about this?" Beth whispered.

"He likes you." Danny adjusted her lapels, then stepped back. "Besides, you're pregnant. You aren't allowed to diet."

Beth chuckled. "True enough."

From inside her, the baby hiccuped again, and she smiled and rubbed that spot on the top of her belly. Right now, she and her baby shared these private moments and nobody was the wiser, but soon enough, she'd be in Danny's shoes with a child who reached out to the people around her—for better or for worse.

THE ICE CREAM bowls were in the sink, and there was a scattering of mini marshmallows over the floor that Dan would have to sweep up later. Dan wiped the dribbles off the jar of chocolate sauce and put it back into the fridge.

"Aren't you glad you indulged?" he asked Beth with a grin. She'd had two helpings.

"Yes, for sure." She licked her fingertip. "That was delicious."

Dan poked his head out of the kitchen into the living room, where Luke had been playing on his iPad, and he spotted his son asleep on the floor. He was getting so big, but he still curled up on his side—the same way he'd slept since he was a toddler. The only difference now was that he no longer popped a thumb into his mouth.

"I guess he's worn out," Dan said. "He was up at like five this morning practicing those lines…"

Beth shot him an amused look. "Does that mean you were up at five, too?"

"You tease now," Dan replied. "But in a few short weeks you're going to be up all night."

Beth met his gaze then nodded. "That

is true… Danny, we've come a long way, haven't we?"

Dan glanced around the kitchen—*his* kitchen. The fridge was covered in Luke's stuff—notes from school, a spelling test that he'd aced, an art project where Luke had drawn a self-portrait that Dan thought showed real talent. He'd bought this house, done a few renovations himself and raised his son here. He'd come a long way from being the new guy in town who always wanted to be just a little bit more like the Thomases. He liked who he'd become. He might not be the perfect dad, but he was a darn good one. And he'd put together a stable life for his kid—he was proud of that.

"Yeah, I guess we have." He tossed a dishrag into the sink. "We're well and truly grown-up."

She nodded slowly, running her hands down her stomach. "Being a single parent is hard, isn't it?"

"Hardest thing I've ever done," he agreed.

"But you figured it out," Beth said.

"Yeah, I did. I'm still figuring it out. The big secret is that no parent knows what they're doing that first time around. It's all new. I've never been the dad of an eight-year-old before. I still feel like I'm scrambling."

"That makes me feel a bit better." She leaned against the counter and shifted her weight from one foot to the other. Did her feet hurt? He'd heard of that, at least—pregnant women with sore feet.

"Are you tired?" Dan asked.

"Yeah. I could sit down." She looked pale, and he felt bad.

"Why don't we go to the couch?" Dan suggested. "It's more comfortable."

Beth led the way and lowered herself into the cushion. He couldn't help but smile as he watched the process. She wasn't at her most graceful, but he liked Beth this way. She was more real—more accessible. He sat down next to her, and from where he sat he could see Luke snoring away next to the heating vent.

"I've never done the pregnancy stage of things," Dan said, keeping his voice low so he wouldn't wake his son. "I don't know about this part. If I do something dumb like make you stand for too long, just let me know."

"It's okay." She cast him a smile. "I'm trying to get tougher."

"Why?" He gave her a funny look.

"I need to." She adjusted her position, turning herself toward him. "I'm going to be a single mother, and I'll need to figure all of this out."

"You'll have your dad, though," he countered.

"Yeah..." She smiled wistfully. "I grew up with a novelist father. My daughter will have a novelist grandpa. She'll be lucky that way—exposed to the literary world firsthand."

Dan nodded. "You'll be okay."

"You were right, though," she added. "I'll have to draw a few lines with my dad. I do need his help, but I want to raise Riley my way."

"I was the same," he agreed. "Except I had a whole lot of guilt to add to it. I wasn't there for Lana when Luke was born, or when he was a baby. I was the deadbeat parent for three years, and I had a lot to make up for. At least you'll get to do this from the very beginning."

"But I have no idea what I'm doing..."

Her smile faded. "I've read articles. I hope that's enough."

"That's more than I had." Dan looked over at Luke, who was still snoring deeply. "You know, a lot of it's just trusting your gut. You get to know what upsets your kid, or what bothers him. You figure it out, and the few times that I went against my gut instinct, I always regretted it."

"Yeah?" She pushed a curl away from her eyes. "Like what?"

"Like when I followed some lady's advice on potty training. Luke was still in training pants, and she said he was too old for that and I should just get firm. I tried that. Poor Luke just cried and cried. He was a wreck." He winced, remembering it. "I decided then and there that I didn't need to do it anyone else's way. We'd figure it out together."

"So your advice is to not take advice?"

Dan grinned. "You know me—always the rebel." He paused. "No one knows Luke like I do, and he isn't their job. He's mine."

"I get a fair amount of unsolicited advice already," she said.

"You'll get more." He shot her a grin. "But it gets easier. It's not like I don't look at other parents and try to figure out how they do this stuff. Take the Christmas pageant—"

He was talking too much. What was it about Beth that made him want to open up like this? She'd always had that effect on him, and while he knew it would be better to say less around her, it felt good to have someone who understood his position.

"What about the Christmas pageant?" Her voice was soft, and she tipped her head to the side, waiting.

"I started Luke in that pageant because you told me that your parents had always had you and your brother in it. I don't know…it just seemed like a wholesome thing to do."

"Really?" She smiled. "That was because of us?"

"Well, I thought you turned out pretty well…"

She smiled, blue eyes glittering in the low light, and he smiled back. She'd always been pretty, but her beauty seemed to go deeper now. Maybe this was just plain old biology working its magic on him—the allure of a pregnant woman. But no, it was more than that…

"Your family had what I'd always wanted," he admitted, his voice low and gravelly.

"We weren't perfect," she said softly. "Far from it."

"But you loved each other." The curl fell across her forehead again, and he reached forward to brush it back. Her skin was silky against his work-roughened fingers, and he pulled his hand back.

Beth looked down and rubbed a hand over her belly. "She's got the hiccups."

"Really?" He looked down at her stomach, as if he could see what she felt. Still, it intrigued him. "That happens?"

"Pretty often, actually." She raised her gaze and laughed softly. "It feels kind of funny. Here—"

She reached for his hand. Dan hesitated, then allowed her to guide his fingers over her taut belly. Then she stopped and pressed his hand down. He could feel movement inside her, a wriggle, almost, and then a tiny jump. A pause, then another jump. He grinned.

"That's insane. Hiccups!"

"Yep." She moved his hand to the side of her stomach. "You can probably feel more here…"

He felt what he could have sworn was a foot against his hand. Then another hiccup.

"Does that hurt?" he asked. The movements were quite robust, and that foot had made some real contact with his hand.

"No," she said. "It's just…movement. I mean, sometimes she'll get me in a weird angle or step on my bladder, but most of the time it's not bad. She must have liked the sugar shot from the ice cream."

It was amazing. He'd missed all of this with Luke. It felt intimate, touching her belly, and it dredged up protective instincts inside him that he didn't know what to do with. He hadn't moved his palm, and her cool fingers lingered on his hand as he felt another wriggle.

"Did you feel that?" she asked.

"Yeah…"

"That was a foot, I think," she said. Beth wasn't looking at him. She was looking at her stomach, her lips parted as she waited for the next movement. She had never looked so beautiful…her eyes glistening, her cheeks faintly flushed. With his free hand, he moved her hair away from her face and tucked it behind her ear, and she looked up, her gaze meeting his. He hadn't known what he'd expected to happen, but her lips were so close, and that faint floral scent that she carried around with her seemed to tug him closer still. He knew what he wanted, and he had a sense that he'd regret this a whole lot...

"Danny?" she whispered.

"Yeah?" His voice was gruff.

"I missed you..."

Those words cut through the last of his inhibitions and he finally let go of his control. It was a rush of relief to slide his arms around her again, tugging her closer, kissing her deeply. She was warm and soft in his arms and she kissed him back, her hands clutching the front of his shirt and pulling him closer still. Her belly pressed against him, and his pulse sped up. He'd kick himself for this later, he knew that, but right now it felt so right.

He'd missed her desperately. He'd resented her, even hated her at some points, but she'd left this aching hole when she walked away, and he'd never fully healed. He'd missed this—the feel of her, the scent of her, the tickle of her breath against his face—

Beth was the first to pull back, and he reluctantly let go. His heart was hammering, and he had to shut his eyes to pull himself together.

"Was that my fault?" she whispered, her cheeks coloring.

"Nope. That was all me." He swallowed hard, and his gaze moved down to her plumped lips. If he could only do that again...

"Danny, we shouldn't—"

He knew that. Of course they shouldn't. There were a hundred good reasons not to, and he was sure he'd remember every single one of them once she was out of his house, but right now, he couldn't pin two thoughts together.

"You said you missed me," he murmured.

"I did." She was still near enough that he could easily close that distance between them, but he wouldn't. Beth turned away, and he leaned back with a sigh.

"I'm not thinking straight," she said. "This is just...chemistry."

"I'm not, either." He cast her a wry smile. "Sorry."

"It's late," she said, and she tried to push

herself up but didn't seem able to do it. "Oh, for crying out loud!"

"Need a hand?" Dan asked with a low laugh.

"Please."

He stood up and took her hands in his and gave her a tug to lever her to her feet. "Hard to make an elegant exit when you're stuck in my couch, huh?"

"You have no idea." Her cheeks tinged pink and she shook her head. "I do need to go, Danny."

"I know." He let go of her hands and took a step back. "I'll behave myself."

Dan helped her into her coat and wrapped her scarf around her neck tenderly. Maybe it was chemistry, but it sure was strong. He'd kick himself for this later—that was a given—but she was beautiful tonight.

"Are you going to be able to get out of your car on your own?" he asked as she opened the front door.

"Yes, I've got a system. Your couch is the problem." She stepped out into the winter chill, and her breath froze in the air. He wanted to tug her back inside and kiss her again. He wanted to keep her warm in his arms—

Chemistry. Some biological pull between two healthy adults. That's it—wasn't that their agreement, at least?

"Good night, Beth," he said.

"Good night, Danny."

He watched as she got into her car and drove off, then he shut the door and locked it, waiting for logic and reason to calm his pulse. Then he looked over at Luke, still snoring on the floor, and he heaved a sigh.

It didn't matter what a woman could do to his heart rate if he couldn't trust her to be strong by his side during hard times, too. She couldn't be right for him if he couldn't trust her to be the rock that Luke needed, too. That was part of being a parent...

And there it was—the rush of regret he'd been expecting.

CHAPTER TWELVE

BETH STOOD IN a secondhand-jewelry shop in downtown North Fork. The shops were busy, Christmas music playing in every store. The sun was shining, but a few snow-flakes fell nonetheless, sparkling in the air as they floated to the ground. She'd hoped that some shopping would take her mind off Danny, but so far it hadn't worked.

She'd replayed that kiss over and over all last night, remembering the feeling of his arms slipping around her, the softness of his lips… That wasn't the old Danny she'd felt in that embrace. This was the mature man with his restraint and urgency battling each other.

There was something deeper and more insistent about this kiss than their last one. He'd known what he wanted, and if she hadn't pulled back when she did— A blush burned her cheeks. That kiss was more trou-bling than their last, because it had overridden all the logic that she had thought would protect her. They'd known better. What were they doing—what was *she* doing? Even the memory of his lips moving over hers sped up her heart. Those conflicting feelings had their root in their past relationship, but that kiss had been very much in the present.

She'd made a large enough mistake the night her daughter was conceived, and at this point she was supposed to know better than to just give herself up to a moment and live to regret it later. Actions had consequences—maybe especially now that she was pregnant. And she knew better than to toy with emotions that went that deep. Passion, heartbreak, regret…this wasn't a game, and Danny wasn't just some stranger in a bar. He was the guy who could tangle up her emotions like no one else.

In the secondhand-jewelry shop, Beth had found a locket that Granny could put a picture of Grandpa in and wear around her neck. The wind stung her cheeks as Beth stepped outside, her bags at her side. Those few snowflakes still sparkled in the air, sunlight illuminating them in winter magic. It was like seeing the sun shine and rain fall at the same time—rare, but it happened, and she always stopped to enjoy the phenomenon. Except today was too cold, so Beth headed down the sidewalk. She realized that she had one more gift she wanted to buy... for Danny.

Except that wasn't appropriate. Just because they'd been close once didn't mean that exchanging Christmas gifts wouldn't be weird now. Even with their recent struggle with their attraction for each other—which was best put solidly behind them. And if she bought something for Danny, she'd need to get something for Luke, too. And that wasn't a problem, except that it stopped being a nostalgic gesture and started being something different. Something tangible and present, and she wasn't trying to make any statements or put Danny in an awkward position.

I'm hormonal, she reminded herself. *I'm more emotional than I would be.*

That was it, wasn't it? That could also explain her passionate response to Danny's kiss last night, because that certainly hadn't been logical. It couldn't exactly explain *his* kiss, though... Was she completely overthinking this?

"Yes," she said aloud. She was. This was ridiculous. He'd kissed her. She'd kissed him back. Again. It was another mistake—they both knew that—the end! She had bigger problems and bigger responsibilities to worry about than *a couple of kisses*. They were just learning how to coexist in the same town.

Beth waited at a curb until a car had passed, then she crossed the street. On the corner there was a cozy bistro, and she thought she might stop in for a bite to eat. As she approached, she scanned the patrons through the front window. She'd always enjoyed doing that—watching people eat—but as her gaze fell on a table a little way back, she stopped short. Her father sat at that table, his sleeves rolled up to his forearms, a bowl of soup in front of him, and across the table from him sat Linda. They didn't see Beth—they were looking at each other, deep in conversation. It wasn't a look of love, exactly—more a look of intense, earnest listening. She paused, watching them, her heart thumping in her chest.

What was this, exactly? Was her father

on a date? Or were they just hammering out mutual interests?

"Hi."

Beth startled and looked up to find Danny standing next to her. His cheeks were reddened from the cold, and he smiled.

"Hungry?" he asked.

"No." She'd answered faster than she meant to, and it wasn't even true. She was starving, but she wasn't going inside. She turned away from the window, heat flooding into her cheeks.

"You okay?" Danny eyed her speculatively.

"My dad's in there." She licked her lips. "With Linda."

Danny looked over her head, and she glanced back to see both her father and Linda looking away from the window and toward the waiter. It was just as well. She'd rather not be caught spying.

Beth started walking again. Linda and Dad—together. Her father hadn't mentioned that Linda was still in town. Beth had assumed that she'd gone home to Edmonton again. But apparently, she had not. Why was her father keeping secrets like that? Not that it was her business…

"You are hungry, aren't you?" Danny said, matching her pace easily.

"Sort of," she admitted. "I'm always hungry these days."

"How about the bakery? I'll buy you a doughnut."

"Buy me a full sandwich and you have a deal." She cracked a smile.

"Done."

Danny put a hand on her elbow as they crossed the street, and she found herself oddly comforted by the gesture. She tugged her scarf higher on her chin to fend off the wind, and when they got to the curb, there was a puddle of salt-melted slush awaiting them. Danny took her hand firmly in his and helped her across it. Granted, in her condition, she needed the extra help, but once on the sidewalk again, she pulled her hand free.

"Thank you," she said. But she couldn't do this—lean on Danny as if he were more than just an old friend. Her emotions needed some clear lines—gray areas weren't going to work. Not right now.

Danny didn't say anything, but he gave

her some space as they walked toward the bakery, and when he opened the door for her, she looked back at the bistro across the street. Seeing her father with Linda had been unsettling—too much like the old days, she supposed. They used to go out to eat at that bistro on their date nights.

Danny ordered Beth a turkey sandwich and a couple of doughnuts for himself. Then they took their tray and headed for a table by the window. Beth put her bags down beside her chair and eased into the seat. She needed more room now to make space for her stomach, and she rubbed her belly as the baby stretched.

"I wanted to apologize for last night," Danny said as he sat.

"It's okay," she said.

"Not really," he said. "I know you're in a vulnerable spot right now, and I keep forgetting that."

Beth nodded, then felt her cheeks heat. "It wasn't only you, Danny."

Her mind went back to the way she'd clutched the front of his shirt, holding him there, holding him close...not wanting that kiss to end. She was most certainly culpable, too.

"Well…I started it." He smiled uncertainly.

Had he? She wasn't even sure. She'd been the one to tell him how she was feeling—missing him the way she had. She shouldn't have done that—some things were better left unsaid. It had been a mixture of low lights and low voices…

"I can't play games," she admitted quietly. "I'm having a baby…my life is upside down, I'm emotional, it's Christmas—" Beth clamped her mouth shut, trying to sort out the words.

"I know," he replied. "I feel the same way. When I'm with you, I forget all of the excellent reasons to keep things—" he shrugged "—kosher, I guess."

"We know there's an attraction between us," she said. "I thought that just admitting it would help, but—"

"Yeah, it didn't do much, did it?" His gaze was warm, safe. But she wouldn't be pulled in. She had to keep her head on straight, and Danny had always been able to turn her upside down with his lopsided smile.

"So we should be more careful," she said.
"Yeah…"

"I'm pregnant because I did something stupid without thinking," she said earnestly. "I'm not going to make a mistake like this again."

"I know. I wasn't—" Danny looked away, his gaze moving over the icy streets. "We both have kids to put first now."

That covered it. They weren't free to follow their impulses anymore. There were more hearts in the balance than just their own. And it wasn't fair to drag children through an emotional mess just because two adults thought it might be worth some risk. Beth would be careful with her little girl. She wouldn't bring just anyone into her life, and she would make sure that Riley knew that she came first every step of the way.

"So what's the plan?" Danny asked.

Beth sighed. "The plan was to come home and raise my daughter. I want her to have a life here with her grandpa and extended family. North Fork is a beautiful place to grow up—I want her to have this." She eyed him for a moment, then smiled ruefully. "You being here complicates that, though."

"Yeah?" He didn't look daunted. "This town isn't big enough for the both of us?"

"It'll have to be, won't it?"

"I'll behave," he said with a small smile.

"So you keep saying." She chuckled. "We'll figure it out, I'm sure."

"But what about a job?" he asked. "Any thoughts there?"

"Once my maternity leave is up, I was thinking it would be nice to get back into caring for the elderly. In fact, I could apply to be a caregiver for Granny through the government support channels. She'll need a caregiver soon, and I'd rather it be me than anyone else."

"So you really do have plans. Here."

Was that uncertainty she heard in his voice? Was her presence here cramping his style? They'd have to sort out their ill-fated chemistry some way or other, because this was her home, just as much as it was his. She'd been born and raised here.

"This is where I want to raise Riley," she said, then shook her head. "And I'm not making my plans because of what might be fun—I'm looking at what's best for my daughter and my family. That's one mistake I won't be making."

She picked up the sandwich and pulled back the paper. Her stomach rumbled in response.

"Thank you for this," she added. "I appreciate it."

DAN WATCHED AS Beth took a jaw-cracking bite of the sandwich. Crumbs of the crusty bun littered the table in front of her. She was hungry—he could tell by the way she devoured her food. His anxiety mounted as he considered her words: she was staying in town. It wasn't that he wanted her to go, because he seemed to be wanting a whole lot more from her lately, but it might be good for him if she did. He'd find his balance again, at least. With her here...

His mind went back to that kiss the night before. There had to be some middle ground—making peace with her without crossing those lines. They'd be living in the same town, after all, and running into each other from time to time. They couldn't just become strangers again and erase their past, either. Besides... Looking at her, his heart softened. She needed someone looking out for her. She was having a baby and resolutely charging forward as she did with everything, but she wasn't as invulnerable as she thought.

All he knew was that Beth didn't have a partner at her side to help her over puddles or catch her if she fell. Beth acted like she had everything under control, and he knew she'd never admit to needing a hand, but pregnancy wasn't easy, and neither was being a single mom to a newborn. He'd messed up with Lana, but back then he'd still had a lot of growing up to do. He was more mature now, and he wouldn't let Beth struggle on her own.

Danny finished his doughnut just as Beth polished off her sandwich. He pushed the second doughnut toward her with a small smile.

"That's for you," he said.

"No, really—"

She wanted it, though. He could tell by the way she eyed it.

"I bought the second one for you," he reassured her. "You're eating for two."

Beth grinned and accepted his gift.

"Thanks." She heaved a happy sigh and took a nibble from one side.

"So what's happening between your dad and Linda?" he asked.

"Your guess is as good as mine." She licked her finger. "She came by the other day to give him half of their investments, which was really decent of her. But I thought she'd gone back to Edmonton. I had no idea she was still in town."

Danny nodded. It wasn't his business, but he was curious. "They say breakups are complicated."

Or maybe it wasn't the breaking up that was complicated, but the seeing each other again afterward. Feelings didn't just disappear when a relationship ended. They bled and ached and healed over somewhat, and given half a chance, they kept trying to go back to what they used to be. Even if that wasn't possible. Even if neither person wanted to go back.

"They do say that…" Her tone softened, and she sighed.

"Maybe it's just like us," Dan said. "They have history, and maybe some chemistry still. Maybe they'll remain friends."

"Friends?" She looked up dubiously.

"You don't think that's possible?" he asked, and he felt that old ache in his heart again.

"I think it's possible, but looking back on everything they've put each other through, I'm not sure it's likely."

Yeah, he was afraid of that. After the way Beth left him, maybe it was unrealistic of him to want to keep something with her, too. He'd protect his son at all costs, but was he wrong to want something with her anyway? Not romance—he knew better than that— but not a complete goodbye, either. Beth's gaze flickered up to his face, then down to the last of the doughnut in her hand.

"Dad loves her, Danny."

"Yeah." Dan had seen that, too. He could sympathize. He'd been in love with a woman who couldn't take on someone else's child. It changed what was possible between the two of them, but it didn't erase their feelings. Not all of them.

"And she's in love with him, too—" Beth popped the last of the doughnut into her mouth and chewed thoughtfully. "If it weren't for me, they'd have been a good match."

Dan sighed. "I doubt they see it that way."

Beth shrugged. "They might. Even so, I'm an adult now. If they want to try their marriage again, I'm not a kid anymore. He has to live his life."

"Do you think that's what this is?" Dan asked cautiously.

"No… I don't know. Maybe?" Beth shook her head. "Honestly, at this point, I might be able to appreciate what Linda could offer."

"Yeah?" Dan eyed her in surprise.

"She might be stiff and overly polite, but she does know a lot about social niceties, she gives a thoughtful gift card and she seemed to make my dad happy." Her eyes misted at those last words. "And he's so lonely, Danny…"

Lonely. Yes, Dan supposed that Rick was. Dan was, too, for that matter. He hadn't realized how much he missed sharing his life with someone until Beth had come back to town and awakened something inside him. But he missed *her*. He'd thought that being a dad would be enough—at least for a few years—but Rick proved a powerful point.

Parenthood couldn't fill that void, even if exhaustion might make it easier to ignore. If Beth wasn't the woman for him, then maybe it was time to start looking around for someone else who could be. But with her in town, every other woman seemed to pale in comparison. When she'd walked out on him, they were five days away from their wedding, and in his heart, he'd already taken those vows. For some blasted reason, they'd stuck.

"I hoped that having me at home would help Dad cheer up," Beth went on. "And a grandbaby—that would shake things up! But, it isn't the same, is it?"

"He'll be okay," Dan said. "Even if it isn't Linda, he'll find someone again."

Beth wiped her fingers on the napkin, then gave Dan a sad smile.

"He will, and I'll have to move out to give him that space. I'll need the space, too, but it'll be nice to have him close by, at least."

Dan glanced at his watch.

"I don't have too much time," he admitted. "I've got to shop for Luke's Christmas gift."

"What will you get him?" Beth asked, tidying the table.

"I don't know," Dan said. "He's at an awkward age. He's still a kid, but trucks don't cut it anymore."

All Luke had asked for Christmas this year was to have his mom back in some form, and that was too big a Christmas wish. If only they could go back to the years of shining eyes and dreams of monster trucks. At least that was doable. But if Luke was starting to wish for a mom, maybe it was time for Dan to start looking at what he needed in a relationship, too. Beth might be hard to get over, but he'd never manage it if he didn't at least try.

"You'll figure him out," Beth said, rising to her feet. "You're his dad. It's what you do."

"Yeah, it's what I do." He nodded, and Beth took the wrappers to the garbage can by the door. She hitched her purse up onto her shoulder and raised her hand.

"Thank you for lunch, Danny. I'll let you get back to shopping."

He noticed her bags beside the chair.

"Beth, wait—" He scooped them up and met her at the door.

"Thanks." Her cheeks colored, and her hand lingered in his as she took the bags. Her perfume mingled with the bakery scents, and he wished with all his heart that this could be easier.

"Merry Christmas, Beth," he said softly.

And she smiled as she headed back out onto the sidewalk. Danny stood there for a moment, watching her walk away.

All Luke wanted for Christmas was his mother, and all Dan seemed to want was the beautiful blonde who smiled up into his eyes and called him "Danny." He and Luke would both be out of luck. Lana wasn't coming back, and that was for the best. She couldn't be the mother that Luke imagined, or even needed. And Beth couldn't be that mother, either.

Ever since Beth had come back to town, a wish had started to grow in Dan's heart, too—a mom for Luke who could finally fill that aching gap in his own heart, too. He and his son had the same longing for a woman who could be their everything. But Christmas wishes didn't always come true.

That was why there was New Year's right after Christmas—to wash away that disappointment and to give everyone a fresh start.

Every New Year's Eve, Dan made the same resolution: to be a better dad. It was the only thing he seemed to be able to control.

CHAPTER THIRTEEN

CHRISTMAS EVE WAS two days away, and Beth couldn't believe how quickly the time was passing. She and her father had finished their breakfast, and they were sitting in the living room looking at the Christmas tree. So many ornaments from when Mom was alive…and a few still on the tree that Linda had chosen. Beth might not have appreciated her step-mother as a teen and young adult, but she had a new sympathy for her difficult position now. Rick sat on the couch, flicking through the TV channels.

"Pick a channel, dear. You'll give me a stroke," Granny said quietly. She'd been lucid all morning.

"Channel surfing doesn't bring on strokes, Mom," Rick said with a wry smile.

"And wouldn't you feel awful if you were wrong." Granny shot him an arch look, and Beth chuckled.

"It's a seizure, Granny," Beth said. "Strobe lights can cause them, that kind of thing."

"Even worse," Granny retorted.

Rick rolled his eyes at Beth. "You're no help."

"Not trying to be," Beth replied with exaggerated sweetness. "I want answers. What's going on with you and Linda?"

"Nothing is going on." Her father sighed. "We had lunch. We talked. Not that it's your business, Beth. We were married for twenty years, and that takes some time to unravel."

Not her business. She knew that, but she worried about her father all the same.

"Do you miss her?" Beth asked.

Her father gave her a long look, then asked, "Do you miss Dan?"

"Yes," she said. "I can admit that. I do."

"And do you want to talk about that?" her father asked pointedly.

"No." She gave him a small smile. "Not really."

He pointed at her with one finger. "Bingo, kiddo."

Fine. Her dad had always kept his relationship with Linda private, and maybe that was proper. What place did a young teen have in her father's marriage anyway? He'd been the parent, and she'd been the child. That was how her father had always run their home. But she could see that living here as an adult with her father wouldn't be easy.

"Dad, I'm going to find my own place soon. I mean, I'll probably wait until the baby arrives to make the move easier, but I think we could both use a bit more privacy."

"What?" Her father frowned. "No! You're going to need a whole lot more support than you think."

The support she was missing was that of a husband, not her father's. She knew she could count on her dad, but if she was going to move forward, she'd need to be on her own two feet.

"Come on, Dad. I'm in your way, and you know it."

"This is your home, Beth." Her father shook his head and pushed himself to his feet. "That doesn't change. It never did! This has always been your home."

Rick stalked out of the room, and Beth leaned her head back against the couch. Her home...yes, it had been, but it had been a long time since she'd felt at peace here.

"What's going on with Linda?" she asked her grandmother.

"I have no idea," Granny said. "But he's right, you know."

"About me minding my own business?" Beth asked with a low laugh.

"About this being your home," Granny replied. "You might have been angry as a teenager, but you knew where you belonged."

She had known where she belonged, but she'd also felt like she had to fight to keep her place. It had been a complicated time, and maybe that had been partly because of her age, and partly because she and Linda had never bonded...

Beth pushed herself to her feet. "I'm going to take a walk, Granny."

"All right, dear. Be careful on that ice." Granny looked up with a smile. "If you see Grandpa, ask him what he wants for lunch."

Beth froze. The boundary line between lucidity and confusion tended to blur, and Beth never quite saw it coming. Her heart squeezed in sadness. It always felt like a goodbye somehow when Granny slipped back into the past.

"Actually, he left something for you—hold

on." Beth went upstairs to where she'd put the old note that Danny had found in the desk at the store. She came back down with it and passed it to her grandmother.

"A shopping list?" she asked with a short laugh, but then she saw the note at the bottom. "Oh, that charmer." A smile spread over Granny's face. "Thank you, dear."

Beth had been saving the note for a time like this, and it seemed to bring sincere happiness to her grandmother.

But Beth needed to get out of the house. She needed some space to think and some air to breathe. Coming home had seemed like the solution when she was in Edmonton, trying to figure out how to raise a baby alone, but now that she was back, she could see that it wouldn't be quite so simple. She was still the strong-willed daughter, and her father was still...her father. They'd be adding an infant to the mix—that was all. She needed to think, and a walk would do her some good.

"So you stay here and wait, okay, Granny?" Beth said. "I'm sure he'll be back soon."

"Of course, dear," Granny said, as if the

very thought of anything else were absurd. Beth chuckled and shook her head. She headed for the back door where her coat and boots were and put them on. When her daughter arrived, she knew she'd need help, but the two of them would also need their own space. If Beth was going to be a caregiver to her grandmother, she'd also need a home to retreat to, a place to rest and recharge. Boundaries were important, but sorting this out wasn't going to be easy.

As Beth walked, she wondered just how much had actually changed. Danny was still in town, and she could have dealt with that easily enough if their attraction had stayed in the past. Memories could be difficult, but as Danny pointed out, she'd be making new memories with her daughter. Except what they seemed to be feeling for each other wasn't just left over from the past... that kiss had nothing to do with her old feelings for her ex-fiancé and everything to do with the stoic, sweet guy she'd been spending so much time with lately. That disturbed her. Was she developing feelings for Danny *again*?

Beth paused at the corner and let out a

Why did she have to fixate on this year of history? Dan wasn't marrying her granddaughter, and he'd never make those marriage vows to her. That was in the past, but what was he supposed to do—break Granny's heart over and over again?

Besides, Beth was the one who'd needed the refresher on wedding vows and standing by her man. She was the one who'd taken off the minute things got hard. She was the one who'd turned her back on him and his son. He hadn't been the one confused about commitment—that was Beth, and frankly, he was tired of pretending with Granny. She was muddled, but this was the present, and Beth was the one who'd walked out on him.

"I understand the importance of commitment, Granny," he said carefully. "Trust me—I do. When two people get married, they'd better be willing to ride out the hard stuff."

"Good." Granny nodded. "I feel better. You're a good man, Daniel."

Dan felt tears in his eyes. She'd always seen the best in him, this sweet old lady, and if things had worked out differently, he'd have been honored to be her grandson.

"Granny," he said quietly. "You remember that Beth is pregnant, right?"

"Yes, and ticktock on that wedding," she said, arching one eyebrow.

Ticktock, indeed. "She's in the hospital now, having the baby. I have to pick up my son from school, and then we could go out for supper while we wait. What do you think?"

"My goodness!" Granny leaped to her feet. "That's exactly what we need to do! Oh, my…what should I bring… What will she need?"

Granny rushed past him into the kitchen. He heard drawers opening and closing, and he went to the doorway, watching her. She had pulled out a ladle and a can opener and she was staring at them in confusion.

"We don't need to bring anything, Granny," he said softly. "She's got everything she needs. Rick is with her. We're just waiting for him to call us. That's it."

He wasn't a part of this any more than Beth was part of his problems. Why did that hurt a little to admit?

"Are you sure?" Granny asked uncertainly.

"I'm positive," he said with a nod. "All you need is your boots and your coat. How does pizza sound? Or we could do that new Chinese place."

"Oh!" Granny smiled again. "Have you seen Ralph?"

Dan suppressed a groan. It was going to be a long evening, but maybe it was just as well. Waiting would be harder still without the distraction.

"He went for milk, Granny," Dan said. "I'm sure we'll run into him later."

"Milk." Granny nodded, then sighed. "All right. Boots, you say, and a coat."

They were headed in the right direction. Dan would have to take it.

CHAPTER FIFTEEN

BETH HAD THOUGHT that she'd have a little more time to prepare before delivering her baby, but that was not to be. After she got to a room, the nurses took over and Beth found herself briskly changed into a hospital gown and settled into a bed. It was all happening so quickly that Beth couldn't help the panic that threatened to overwhelm her. Today? It seemed impossible, and yet it was bearing down on her whether she was ready or not.

The contractions continued over the next few hours, and as the pain swept over her, her dad stayed by her side. Rick sat by her head, refusing to move as Beth labored.

"Doing good, Beth," the nurse said as she checked her progress. "We're almost there. It's going to be time to push on the next contraction, okay?"

"No!" Beth gasped.

"Oh, yes," the nurse replied with a low laugh. "You'll do fine. Breathe now."

"Dad, I'm not ready for this!" Beth said, turning toward her father. His face was ashen, but he seemed much calmer than she felt.

"Sure, you are," Rick said, taking her hand. "You're already doing it…"

"I mean…" Tears welled in her eyes. "I mean, being a mom—"

"No one's ready for that," her father said. "Your mom and I weren't ready for it, either. You can plan all you want, you're never ready."

Was that the case? Because she felt like she needed more time, more advice, more plans laid so that she could do this properly. She needed backup plans, and just-in-case scenarios…

"I don't know how to do it alone," she whispered.

"You aren't alone, kiddo." Her father tightened his grip on her hand. "You've got me, okay? You're my little girl, and I'm going to be here no matter what."

Another contraction swept over her, and Beth shut her eyes against the pain, everything else evaporating around her. Her body squeezed and Beth struggled to pull in a breath…

"Push!" she heard the nurse say, and her father's hand tightened on hers as she did as she was told. The pain was overwhelming, and she lifted her head, pushing through the pain and the fear. It felt like it would never end, but then it subsided, and she dropped back against the bed, gasping for air.

"Okay, this next one is going to do it, Beth," the nurse said. "You're almost there, okay?"

For the next few minutes, as Beth pushed through the most searing agony she'd ever experienced, she listened to the voice of the nurses as they cheered her on. She squeezed her father's hand and heard his low voice beside her.

"Come on, Beth. Good girl. You're doing it! Come on, Beth!"

"We've got the head!" the nurse said. "Oh my goodness, the hair on this baby. Your baby has a full head of hair, Beth! One more push—"

The pain peaked, and then there was the sound of a baby's wail, the nurses' cheer, and it was over. Beth fell back against the pillow, tears streaming down her cheeks.

"It's a girl!" the nurse said. "You've got a healthy baby girl…"

Beth strained to see her baby, and in a moment, a tiny bundle wrapped loosely in a warmed blanket was placed on her stomach, and Beth felt a flood of relief.

Her baby…her daughter. Beth waited while someone cut the umbilical cord, and then she pulled her baby up into her arms and looked down into the squished little face.

"Hello, Riley," she whispered. "I'm your mommy."

Beth looked up at her father to see tears in his eyes. He bent down and pressed a kiss against Beth's forehead.

"Good job, kiddo," he said gruffly. "You did great."

Riley was so small. She had a shock of wet black hair, and a button nose. Her eyes were squeezed shut, but she opened them a crack when Beth leaned over her. And as Beth looked down into the face of her newborn baby, she felt a swell of love like nothing she'd ever felt in her life. It came from deep inside her and welled up like a tidal wave of protectiveness.

"What are you naming her?" the nurse asked.

Beth had been planning on giving Riley Granny's name as a middle, but looking down at her, she knew better. Beth ran a finger down her daughter's hand. "Her name is Riley Anne Thomas."

"Anne, after your mom," her father said, a smile in his voice.

Beth nodded. It only seemed right to honor her mother in some way. She'd have wanted to be here for this—her granddaughter's birth.

"I think it's perfect," Rick said, and she heard the emotion catch in his voice, but Beth's eyes were still fixed on her baby. She wanted to memorize every detail of her face, her hands and feet. She'd felt this little girl moving around on the inside for months now, and every time, she'd wondered what she'd look like. Now that she knew, it seemed almost surreal.

"Dad—" Beth looked over to her father. "I'm going to find my own place as soon as I can."

"Beth…" Rick shook his head. "Look, you don't need to do that."

"Yes, I do," she said. "I'm a grown woman now, and I think you and I both need our space."

"You might be grown, but you're still my daughter." Her father eased into the chair next to her bed. "I know you want to do this on your own, but you don't have to. I'm not going to stop being your dad or this little one's grandfather. And you don't have to worry about anything. Linda brought me my half of those investments, and I'm going to find a job to keep some money coming in—" He shook his head as Beth opened her mouth. "I'm serious, Beth. You're not alone in this. Riley will have a grandpa who'll be wrapped right around her finger. That's that."

There was time to hash out the details, and Beth turned her attention back to her baby. How many years had she longed to hear that kind of devotion in her father's voice when he spoke to her? How long had she wished that her dad would unconditionally choose *her*? Today, on the day he became a grandfather for the first time, he had.

"I'm a mother..." Beth murmured, in awe.

"And I'm a grandpa." Her father chuckled. "I should probably make some calls. I'll be back in a few minutes, okay?"

"Okay..."

Her father left the room, and Beth pressed her lips against her daughter's soft forehead. She'd choose Riley first, every time. She'd put her daughter's needs ahead of her own. She'd protect her baby with every breath, and she'd never let her child doubt her love—not for a single second. Riley was going to be her top priority for the rest of Beth's days.

For the next hour, Beth had time alone with her daughter. She'd meant to stare into her little girl's face the entire time, but her energy was spent, and she fell into an exhausted slumber. A while later, the hospital room door opened once more, and Rick poked his head in.

"Beth, there are some people here to see you. You up to it?"

"Sure," Beth said, and the door opened farther to reveal Granny. The old woman's face erupted into a wreath of smiles, and she was followed by Danny and Luke. Luke hung back, and Danny stood by the door, letting Granny go first. Beth's gaze moved back to Danny—standing there with his eyes locked on her tenderly, as if she were the one who'd just been born. And perhaps she had been—a newborn mother.

Granny tutted and oohed and aahed over Riley, then straightened and shot Danny a severe look.

"Daniel," she said reprovingly. "Come over here and meet your daughter."

Danny paled first, then he smiled uncomfortably. Granny was settled in the past, it seemed, and Beth had to laugh. It was ridiculous, this balance of caring for Granny's dementia, and sometimes there was no other reaction.

"It's okay," Beth said. "Come see her."

"Why don't I take Luke and Granny down to the cafeteria for a few minutes?" Rick suggested, and Beth nodded. It might be easier that way… She was still tired, and it would be easier if they weren't all playing along with Granny's version of reality. Right now, Beth needed the real world.

Granny pottered toward the door, but when she got to Danny, she took his hand in hers and looked up into his eyes.

"Daniel," she said firmly, "that wedding needs to happen pronto. Ticktock."

DAN MET GRANNY'S GAZE, and he could have sworn she was lucid. She looked like she was in the here and now, but he knew she had to be stuck in the past. He licked his lips.

"I understand, Granny," he said seriously.

"Good." She patted his hand, then turned to Luke. "Let's get you fed, young man."

In the present or the past, Granny could be counted on to feed whoever was near her. Luke looked at Dan questioningly. Dan hadn't planned what he'd say, exactly, but he knew he wanted a few minutes alone with Beth. But then, that's all he seemed to want lately, whether it was good for them or not.

"Go on down with Mr. Thomas," Dan said, digging in his pocket for some money. He pulled it out and handed it over to his son. "Get some fries or something. I'll just be a few minutes, okay?"

Luke nodded, significantly cheered up by the sight of a twenty.

"Okay," he said. "'Bye, Dad."

Rick, Granny and Luke stepped into the hallway, and Dan watched them head toward the elevator before he went all the way into Beth's room and let the door swing shut behind him. The nurses had gone for the time being, and Dan stood there, his mouth dry as he stared at Beth.

Her golden hair fell in loose curls around her shoulders. Her exhaustion was clear, but her eyes sparkled with a deeper emotion than he'd ever seen. This was it—he was witnessing her life change forever. Beth Thomas was officially a mother now.

"Hi," he said quietly, and Beth smiled.

"Do you want to come see her?" she asked. "Meet my little girl."

Dan crossed the room then sank onto the bed next to Beth, peering into the sleeping face of the newborn. Was this what it had been like when Luke came into the world? He wished with all his heart he hadn't missed that day. The birth of a child was a milestone, an event that changed a person into a parent.

"She's beautiful," Dan said with a slow smile. "Just like her mom."

"You have to say that," Beth said with a chuckle. "And she is beautiful, but I'm a wreck."

"You're a warrior," he countered. "You just had a baby, Beth."

"Can you believe that?" She smoothed a hand over her daughter's hair. "I already can't remember what it was like without her…"

Dan nodded. "I've never seen a baby this new before… I wish I had, though."

Beth didn't answer, not that he'd expected her to. It wasn't up to her to let him off the hook for his past mistakes. He'd have to live with having turned his back on his pregnant girlfriend, whether she'd wanted him involved or not. He should have been there for his son from the very start.

Beth looked up at Dan uncertainly. "Do you want to hold her?"

Dan froze for a moment, then nodded. "Yeah. Can I?"

"Sure."

Dan gingerly took the baby from her and stared down at the tiny person, the slight weight of her in his arms. As he looked down into the wee face, the baby opened her eyes and blinked at him a couple of times.

"Hi there…" he whispered.

The baby shut her eyes again, and Dan felt a lump rise in his throat. She was so perfect.

"I can't believe how small she is," he breathed.

Beth nodded. "I know. They say it doesn't last long, though."

"Yeah…" Dan felt his eyes mist, and he blinked it back. This moment right here with a woman he'd never stopped loving and the baby she'd just delivered—this was what it was all about. The surge of emotion he felt toward her, the protectiveness he felt toward this brand-new baby… It didn't matter who had fathered this child. She was here, and her arrival had thrown off all the veils and masks and shown him exactly what he wanted.

"I want this, Beth," he said quietly as he handed the baby back to her. He met her gaze, then shrugged helplessly.

"You mean you wish you'd had it with Luke…" Beth's clear blue eyes clouded slightly, then she looked down at her daughter again.

"No," he admitted. "I mean, yes, I do wish I'd been there for Luke's birth, but I mean I want this…with you."

Beth stared at him. "What?"

"I'm serious, Beth." Dan swallowed. "Granny lectured me earlier today when I stayed with her while you were here, and…" Dan rested his hand on her leg over the covers. "She said that for our wedding, we needed to use the old-fashioned vows. She said there was a reason that people vowed for better or for worse, for richer or for poorer, in sickness and in health."

"I never liked the obedience part," Beth said with a small smile.

"Me neither." He smiled, then licked his lips. "But she was obviously stuck in the past again, and she wanted me to promise her that no matter what happened with you—sickness, poverty, anything—that I'd love you and never stop. And I *can* promise that." He looked at Beth, silently begging her to understand. "I didn't have to try or vow or—" He shook his head, searching for the words. "Beth, I never stopped loving you."

Love—yes, that was it. He hadn't fully realized it until the words came out, but he still loved her, and he probably hadn't stopped. He'd been angry and betrayed and had desperately wanted to move on, but there had always been an ember in his heart that was just for her.

"I should have stopped," he said, his voice shaking. "Five years—I should have brushed you off after you left and gotten over you. I *should* have."

"Yes," she agreed, but her voice wavered, too. "And you still should."

If only it were that easy—a choice, a decision. A vow, even! It wasn't about choosing her or wanting her—it went deeper, down to his bones.

"I can't," he admitted. "I've tried so hard to just stamp it out, but I loved you when I was a newbie millwright who wanted to marry you, and I loved you when you walked away. I was angry and hurt, and you have no idea how hard I worked to cover it up, to stop feeling anything when I thought about you… So when you showed up again, it was all still there, waiting."

Dan rubbed his hands over his face. "Granny said we needed to make those old-fashioned vows because life could be hard, and we needed to remember what we were promising. But, Beth, I didn't need vows with you to make that a reality. You owe me nothing, and I still can't stop loving you!"

A tear escaped and he wiped it away with the heel of his hand. If only life could be governed by vows and decisions, he'd be able to get his heart back under control. Dan reached across the bed, and she reached back, twining her fingers with his.

He moved closer, then tipped his head down to touch hers.

"I love you, too," she whispered, and that was all it took. He covered her lips with his and kissed her long and slow. When he finally pulled back, her eyes were still shut and a tear slipped down her cheek.

"But we can't…" Beth's eyes fluttered open, and she met his gaze with agonizing directness. "Danny, it isn't Luke, because I could embrace him. He's a sweet boy who needs love. It's us—no matter how nice it would be to give our kids a family, that family would be built on our relationship. We'd have to trust each other, and I don't think we do."

"You still don't trust me?" he asked in disbelief. "I've grown a lot over the past few years, Beth."

"Your first instinct back then was to hide Luke from me…" She sighed. "I've been in a home where the blending didn't work well, Danny. And we can argue about who was to blame for that, but it was miserable. If you and I weren't connected on the deepest level, it wouldn't work. You guard your turf, Danny. As you should, I suppose, but five years ago, you hid a child's existence from me, and ever since I got back into town, you've been staking your territory, so to speak. Luke is yours—and I need to know my place."

"Beth, I'm a dad…that doesn't mean it couldn't change—"

"Linda wasn't the monster I thought she was," Beth interrupted. "And I can see how easy it might be to slide down into bitterness, and the kids need better than that. Your son deserves to come first. So does Riley."

"And they will," Dan countered.

"Danny, I can't do it." She shook her head. "Back when Luke first arrived, I said that asking me to marry you was one proposal, but asking me to be a stepmother was a completely different one. The thing is, starting out on our own—no kids, no complications—

seemed easier. But to do this, to blend together a family, it takes more than emotion or hopes for the future. It takes some concrete relationship skills. I'd need to know that you'd come to me with anything and everything, and while you might be able to make a promise like that now, it isn't natural for you. And in the thick of things, we go back to our habits."

"Yeah…" He sighed. "You don't trust me enough for this."

Her answer was in her silence. "Maybe you're right. We had our chance five years ago, and we made our choices. I messed up and hid Luke from you, and you made your choice. Time might have passed, but it hasn't changed the basics, has it?"

Five years hadn't changed Beth's decision, either. She was right, of course, that the kids needed to come first. He could wrap his heart around her little girl, but if Beth couldn't trust what they were together, there was no point. She was the stronger one right now—facing the reality of their miserable situation. She couldn't trust him…and he was pushing aside his own issues, too. A vow in a ceremony wasn't magical—it was simply supposed to state what was already between them.

Beth looked up at him again, and he saw the agony in her eyes—the depth of what she was giving up for the greater good. How he loved her...why couldn't love be enough? But it never had been, especially not between them.

Dan got up. He couldn't stay here—he had to get out, get some space. His chest ached, and he suspected that he'd just have to get used to that feeling, because he wasn't going to stop loving Beth.

"I'm going to go find Luke," Dan said gruffly.

"Okay," Beth agreed. "Danny, you're a good father."

And she would make an excellent mother, and an amazing wife to someone someday— just not him. He crossed the room and opened the door.

Beth had become a mother today, and her life would never be the same. Neither would his. He'd just realized that all the vows in the world couldn't save him from a lifetime of loving the wrong woman.

CHAPTER SIXTEEN

BETH BROUGHT HER daughter home on Christmas Eve. She buckled her into the car seat for the very first time and sat next to her baby in the back seat while her father drove them home. She just couldn't take her eyes off her daughter—she was too amazing, too perfect… She was here now, and Beth felt the weight of her new responsibilities.

That evening, she held her baby girl in her arms, looking at the Christmas tree. Riley snuggled close, one hand poking out of the blanket. She was a quiet baby so far—completely content as long as she was in her mother's arms, not that Beth minded. Being together seemed just about perfect to her.

Granny puttered in the kitchen—she was making Christmas cookies, and Beth was looking forward to having some of those. She might not be pregnant anymore, but she was still hungry. She was feeding a baby now, and that seemed to use up almost as much of her energy.

Beth looked over the familiar decorations on the Christmas tree—the shiny bulbs, the golden bells, a little glass angel that they'd put there in honor of her mother the Christmas after she passed away…but there was a new decoration now, and seeing it brought a smile to Beth's face.

"Baby's first Christmas!" Beth turned to her father and grinned. "When did you get this?"

"A few days ago." Her father shrugged. "It was just in case."

She could tell he was pleased she'd finally spotted it, though. The ornament hung next to another ornament that Linda had bought a few years ago—two moose with Santa hats and noses touching. Beth exhaled slowly. Her father had put that one on the tree, too. Were his thoughts still with his ex-wife?

Her father's phone blipped, and he turned off the sound.

"Who was that?" Beth asked.

"No one."

"It was Linda, wasn't it?" She turned, and her father's cheeks reddened. She was right.

It was Christmas, and the two of them were missing each other. Almost sixty years old, and they weren't that different from Beth and Danny. They loved each other, even if they couldn't seem to make it work.

"It's okay, kiddo," her father said.

"You should call her back," Beth said.

"Why do you say that?" Rick glanced down at his phone, though.

"Because I'm not a child anymore, Dad." She patted Riley's rump. "And while Linda and I didn't connect terribly well, she made you happy. And I want you to be happy."

"You didn't cause the split," he said. "Maybe I should have reassured you of that before."

"I know. I'd been gone for ages by then. It was the store." Beth smiled when her father shot her a look of surprise. "Granny told me."

"Ah." Rick smiled wanly, then he nodded. "We just couldn't make it work."

She had no idea about the tensions in her father's marriage, but she did know how it felt to have her heart broken. She'd cried all that night in her hospital room, sobbed out her grief at making Danny walk away, but she couldn't in good conscience be with him. She'd cried until she had no more tears, and then she'd slept, only to be wakened by her hungry little girl.

"I still think you should call her," Beth said quietly.

"And if we did talk and—" Her father cleared his throat. "I mean, if, perhaps, she came for Christmas dinner tomorrow?"

That's what she'd thought. They missed each other. Maybe there was a way to fix it, after all…now that the store was gone and they'd seen what it was like to live apart.

Beth shot her father a smile. "That would be fine, Dad."

Her father nodded, then rose his feet. "Maybe I'll just go upstairs and make a call—"

Beth watched her dad climb the stairs, and she sighed. Linda might not have been her first choice, but Beth didn't need mothering anymore. She hadn't for a long time. She was a grown woman now, and despite her father's protestations to the contrary, she still wanted to move into her own place as soon as she could. She'd need her own space, too, to raise her daughter and establish her own home.

Beth's arm was getting tired, and she brought Riley over to the bassinet beside the couch and laid her inside. Riley made a discontented moan but didn't wake. Beth smiled to herself. She could see where this was going already, but she didn't care. Not yet.

Beth stood over the bassinet for a couple of minutes watching her daughter sleep. From the kitchen, she could hear Granny's whisk against a bowl while the old woman hummed a Christmas carol. This was a happy home, in spite of it all, Beth realized. Riley would spend many happy hours here, she could tell. Even if only when visiting her grandpa.

The doorbell rang, and Beth headed over to answer it. She pulled open the door and was shocked to see Luke. He was wearing a scarf that he'd obviously tied himself, because the knot at the front of his neck did nothing to stop the cold. He wasn't wearing gloves, either, and Beth looked behind him into the chilly night, scanning for Danny.

"Hi, Luke," she said. "Are you alone?"

She stepped back and beckoned him inside. The boy came in, shivering.

"Yeah," Luke said. His eyes were red, and

she could tell he'd been crying. She bent down and put her hands on his cold cheeks, tipping his face toward hers.

"What's wrong?" she asked.

Fresh tears welled in the boy's eyes, and his lip quivered. "She didn't come." His words were a whisper, and Beth's stomach sank. Lana. He'd asked Santa for his mother—maybe the boy believed in old Saint Nick after all.

"Let's get you warmed up, Luke," she said. "And then you can tell me what happened."

Luke stepped out of his boots and followed her into the living room. He looked silently at the bassinet. He didn't seem to want to talk at the moment, and she realized that he hadn't seen Riley yet. At the hospital he'd been whisked off before he'd had the chance.

"Do you want to see the baby?" she asked.

Luke went closer and stood looking down at Riley.

"She's little," he said quietly.

"Yeah." Beth put an arm around Luke's shoulders. "Does your dad know where you are?"

Luke slowly shook his head, and she sighed. Again. Poor Danny would be a wreck. Her father's footsteps creaked on the stairs, and Beth looked up as he entered the living room.

"Dad, would you mind calling Danny and letting him know where Luke is?" she asked with a wince.

Her father nodded and immediately began scrolling through his phone for Danny's number.

Beth led Luke to the couch and tugged him down next to her. "Now, tell me what happened, Luke."

"It was my mom," Luke said, his voice shaking. "She was on Facebook, and I used my friend's account to talk to her. And she said she would come to see me tonight and I just had to meet her in front of my school. So I told her which school was mine, and she said she'd be there at seven."

Beth's stomach curdled. He'd sneaked out to meet his mother? All of the worst-case scenarios spun through her head, and she glanced at the clock on the wall. It was eight thirty. He'd been out for an hour and a half already. If Lana had shown up, he could have been almost out of the province by now!

"That's so dangerous, Luke," Beth said, trying to keep her voice steady.

"She didn't come." Luke's chin trembled. "I waited and waited. She didn't come…" His face crumpled, and Beth pulled him close and rocked him in her arms.

"Oh, Luke," she said, her own eyes misting. "I'm so sorry, sweetie."

"Why didn't she come?" Luke wept. "Why not?"

Beth didn't know… She knew she was grateful, though, and she knew that Luke would take it as a rejection. All he wanted was his mother to love him, to want him, and when he'd thought she'd finally come back, she'd let him down again.

It would have been kidnapping, legally speaking, if she'd simply picked him up and driven off. The very thought filled her with fury, but Luke didn't need her indignation.

"Luke, your mom isn't the best parent right now," she said quietly. "Your dad is, though. And he loves you something fierce. If you'd just disappeared on him—"

"I only wanted to *see* Mom!" Luke protested. "I didn't want to leave, just to see her. I wanted to give her a hug!"

He was eight, and far too young to understand all the complications.

"I know." Beth smoothed his hair out of his eyes. "And I'm so sorry that she disappointed you. Especially on Christmas."

Luke let out a shuddering sigh.

"You are a special boy, Luke," she went on. "You're funny, and you're talented, and you're particularly handsome, too. I wouldn't make that up. Any mom would be super lucky to have a son as terrific as you. This isn't about you, Luke. You're a great kid. This is about your mom's situation. And it's complicated right now."

Luke raised his tearstained face toward her and whispered, "I wish you were my mom."

Beth's heart gave a squeeze. "No, you don't," she said. "I'm your friend now, so you like me. But if I was your stepmom, I'd have to make you do your homework—" she made a face "—and I'd have to send you to your room if you were rude. I'd make you eat veggies, too. Whole plates of them!"

She was trying to cajole him into smiling, but Luke wasn't responding to her humor.

"At least you'd be here. That's better than my real mom."

At least she'd be here... Did he mean that? What did kids his age know about how they'd feel in different circumstances? When he couldn't get his way, when she couldn't be sweet and soft all the time, when he'd have to share everything that right now he had to himself... And then she'd be the wicked stepmother, and she'd be tired and emotional, and she'd raise her voice to order him to his room, and he'd yell, "You're not my mom, you know!" And one day when he was a teenager, he'd tell his father, "All I want for my birthday is a day with you alone. Without *them*."

But this wasn't even about Luke or how pleased he'd be with her in his life. This was about her and Danny. It didn't matter how much Luke wanted her around if she couldn't trust Danny when things were hard. If she and Danny weren't solid, they wouldn't be the strong, reliable family that Luke and Riley needed. They needed to know they could trust each other with the uncomfortable, unattractive, divisive things in life, or all the challenges of parenting and stepparenting would drive them apart.

She saw headlights swing up her driveway through the living room window. Danny was here to pick up his son. She pulled her hair away from her face and looked down into Luke's teary eyes.

At least you'd be here... This little boy needed a mother.

"I think your dad's here," she said, putting a hand on his cheek. "And he's going to be mad, but that's only because he was probably scared out of his mind when he couldn't find you."

The doorbell rang, followed by a hard thump of a fist. Beth went to the door and pulled it open, then jumped back as Danny strode inside.

"Luke!" His voice boomed through the house, and Riley's wail erupted from the bassinet.

Beth hurried to pick up her baby, and Danny shot her an apologetic look. But she understood. He'd just had a decade knocked off his life with this scare, no doubt.

"I'm sorry, Dad," Luke said, tears welling up again.

"What the hell was that?" Danny rubbed a hand over his eyes, and she could see that the big man was struggling to hold back his own emotions.

"Mom said she would meet me at the school," Luke said. "And I wanted to see her—"

The blood drained from Danny's face, and rubbed a hand over his eyes. His worst fears were running through his mind—she could see it.

"She didn't show up," Beth added.

"Thank God…" Danny grimaced when he saw Luke's face. "Son, if you'd left—"

"I wasn't going to go, Dad!" Tears streamed down Luke's face. "I just wanted to see her!"

Beth knew they'd need time to talk this one through, and she didn't envy Danny. She'd likely be dealing with her own version of it in eight years or so, when Riley started asking about her own father. Beth snuggled her daughter closer.

"Let's go home," Danny said woodenly. "We'll talk about it, okay?"

"Am I in trouble?" Luke asked plaintively.

"We'll talk…"

Beth met Danny by the door while Luke shoved his feet back into his boots.

"He needs to see her," Beth whispered. "He needs to at least see his mom, so he can see why she can't be with him."

Danny's eyes flashed and he shook his head. "After this, she'll never see him! Setting up a meeting behind my back? That's unforgivable."

She knew he was angry, but she could also see what his anger hid from him—his son's need for his mother.

"Danny—" she started, but he raised a hand, silencing her.

"You aren't part of this decision." His tone was strangely quiet. His words sank in, though, and she nodded, swallowing everything she would have said. He was right. He'd wanted them to be a family, and if she'd agreed, she'd be a part of the parenting, too. But she'd said no. These choices were his and his alone to make.

Danny pulled open the door, and Luke followed his dad out onto the snowy walk. Luke turned back and fixed her with a miserable look before Danny barked something and Luke trudged after him toward the car. Beth closed the door after them to keep the draft away from her newborn.

Her heart was heavy and sodden. She sucked in a breath, trying to sort out her feelings, but she couldn't right now. They were all knotted up. She went back into the living room, stood in front of the Christmas tree, and tears blurred her vision, then started to flow. She couldn't hold it back, and great, shuddering sobs shook her shoulders. She loved him—blast it all, she loved that man, but the kids needed more than what she and Danny could provide.

She was doing this for all of them.

DAN BROUGHT LUKE home that evening, and they sat up together for a couple of hours talking. As much as he hated to admit it, Beth was right. Luke needed to know his mom, and Dan needed to find a way to make that happen safely.

"Doesn't she love me?" Luke had asked.

"She definitely loves you," Dan said. "Maybe that's why she didn't come, because saying goodbye would have been too hard."

"I love *her*," Luke whispered.

Dan emailed Lana that night, too, and told

her that he knew about the meeting, and that they needed to sort this out together—no secrets, no sneaking. He wasn't sure if she'd respond or not. He had a feeling that Lana had agreed to see Luke on impulse, but given time to think it through, she'd changed her mind.

Thank God! Dan was so deeply grateful that she'd changed her mind...

But it made all of this harder, because Luke felt his mother's rejection keenly, and when he finally fell asleep that night, Dan was left with a heavy heart.

This wasn't what Christmas was supposed to be. Luke was supposed to be excited about Santa coming...even though he knew Santa wasn't real by this point. But still—tonight was supposed to be about sugarplums dancing through Luke's head, not the heavy reality of a distant mother. He was supposed to be wondering what surprises were waiting for him under the tree, not if his own mother loved him.

While Luke slept, his eyelashes moist from tears, Dan brought the presents out and put them under the tree. They looked paltry— too few. Four odd-shaped boxes wrapped in

Santa paper with drugstore bows. Somehow, even the Christmas tree sparkled a little less. Dan couldn't fix this...

There was a knock on the front door, and he pushed himself tiredly to his feet. He glanced at his watch and saw that it was past eleven. Who would be coming over this late? Dan pulled open the front door and found Granny Thomas. She wore her red parka, a white hat pulled down over her ears, and she held a foil-wrapped plate.

"Granny!" He looked beyond her to the car in the driveway. Rick was behind the wheel, the car still running. Rick looked at him but didn't wave or make any other gesture of recognition.

"May I come in?" Granny asked gently.

"Yes, of course." Dan moved back, and she stepped inside and stomped her boots on the mat. He shut the door behind her and accepted the plate. He peeked under the foil to see shortbread cookies decorated with icing. "Thank you."

"I told Rick that you needed some Christmas treats," Granny said with a smile.

"I appreciate it." He forced a smile in return. "A bit of Christmas cheer in spite of it all."

"How is the little one?" Granny asked.

Dan looked at her uncertainly. Which "little one" did she mean? "Luke's asleep," he said.

"Good." Granny nodded. "Because I need to speak with you…about Beth."

Dan sighed. He didn't have the strength for this. He couldn't sit here and pretend that they were in the past to comfort Granny, because his heart was ripped to shreds, too. How long would they all playact for her? When would enough be enough?

"Granny," he said gently. "Beth and I aren't getting married."

Granny tipped her head to one side, then nodded. "I know."

"Okay—" So she was in the present. That made things easier.

"So, what about Beth?" he asked.

"I still think you should marry her." Granny pulled off her gloves. "And that isn't confusion talking, dear."

"Granny, I told her I loved her—" His voice caught, and he swallowed. "She can't be a stepmother to Luke. He's my world. I can't just—"

Granny put a hand on his arm and silenced him.

"I can't take too long with this, dear," she said. "Rick is waiting for me in the car. So I need you to hear me. Can you do that?"

"Yeah. Sure."

It was the Granny they'd all known and loved—the practical yet sentimental woman who'd always seen the best in Dan.

"Daniel, I'm losing my memory," she said simply. "I slip back to times past... I forget that Ralph is gone. I think people are younger than they really are, and..." She sighed. "I'm losing what is most important to me, Daniel—my memories of the people I love most."

Dan didn't know what to say. He hadn't realized that she understood her situation, and he had no comfort to offer.

"I'm sorry, Granny," he said simply.

"The thing is," she went on, "I'm losing the memories, but I'm not losing the love. Does that make sense?" She shook her head. "I'm going to need you to remember for me, one day. I won't know who you are, and you'll have to hold on to our memories of our friendship by yourself. I'll think you're a stranger. I hate that."

"I'll remember for you," he assured her.

"And I know you will." Granny smiled sadly. "But while I lose the memories that nail me down, the love is still there inside me. The love is more firmly attached, it seems. It's a better anchor. Love isn't a choice, is it?"

Tears filled Dan's eyes, and he shook his head. "No, it doesn't seem to be."

"When I forget the time I'm in, my heart is filled with memories of love, even if the memories themselves are gone. I still have some remnant—like a sticky residue that can't be washed off. I think you understand that kind of love, don't you?"

A sticky residue—unwanted, perhaps, but cemented on. That summed it up pretty well. Dan smiled wryly, but nodded.

"I can't stop loving her, Granny," he admitted. "It's not about vows. It's just a fact."

She smiled. "I know. I also know that you'll never be able to rinse her out of your heart, Daniel. Ever. If that kind of love sticks despite dementia, then believe me—you're stuck."

This was supposed to make him feel better? Dan heaved a sigh. "Thanks for that."

Granny shrugged. "It is what it is, Daniel. Perhaps it's better to accept that and find a way to make it work with her."

"There isn't a way," he said.

"There's always a way." Granny's eyes teared up again. "I watched her cry tonight, Daniel. I watched my granddaughter sob in front of the Christmas tree with her newborn baby in her arms. She loves you, too... And I've lived a lifetime already, dear. I know how rarely a person comes across a love that strong."

She'd cried? His heart sank at that image—Beth weeping in front of her Christmas tree... If she'd let him comfort her, he'd do it. If she'd let him love her—

"What do I do?" he asked helplessly.

"Show her what's inside," Granny said. "You held back before. You hid your deepest regrets from her because you were afraid she'd see you differently. You have nothing left to lose. I'd say open up, dear boy, and show her the mess in there." She reached out and tapped his chest.

"I did. I told her how much I loved her—"

"No, no," Granny shook her head. "Not just the pretty things. Show her all of it, Daniel. Remember those vows? It's not just about health and wealth and happiness. It's about sickness and poverty and pain, too. I know she loves you deeply, but she needs to trust that you won't hold anything back again."

Dan stood there in silence.

"You also need to forgive her," Granny added.

"For leaving me," he said sullenly.

"Yes." Granny put her gloves back on. "And for whatever it is that she's beating herself up about."

Granny pulled open the front door, and Danny watched as she went back out onto the walk.

"What is she beating herself up about?" Danny called after her.

"I have no idea. I thought you might know. Merry Christmas," she called over her shoulder.

It wasn't fair to put all this on his shoulders. He had a son to worry about. He wasn't enough for Luke—no matter how desperately he wanted to be. He was a single dad, doing the job of two, and he *needed* to be enough. Except Luke still longed for the one thing Dan could never be—a mom.

Dan watched Granny get back into the car, and Rick gave him a salute, then backed the car out of the drive.

Dan would wake tomorrow morning and watch Luke open his presents—a game console and a few games, some clothes he needed for school, a couple of books. And he was going to hope that it was enough, even though it wouldn't be. Because presents might be fun, but they didn't take the place of the heart-deep stuff.

They wouldn't take the place of Lana. They wouldn't take the place of a mom— the one thing Dan couldn't be for his son. Like some cemented-on residue—Granny's similes were practical to the core, but true. Lana was cemented into Luke's heart, and Beth was cemented into Dan's.

Unless there was something in Granny's advice to win back Beth's trust after all these years. Staring at the Christmas tree, the few presents underneath suddenly started to look a little more magical, and the lights on the branches sparkled with a twinkle of hope.

Forgiveness...

He knew what he needed to do. It might not work, but at least he'd give it one more try.

CHAPTER SEVENTEEN

CHRISTMAS MORNING, Beth changed Riley, amazed at how tiny a diaper could be. She'd been up several times during the night to feed and change the baby, and this morning she was tired but content. She had her daughter, and that was everything.

Present opening was later than usual—since everyone but Riley was an adult in the house, and they wanted some precious sleep. Linda was due to come for Christmas dinner today, and Beth was actually looking forward to seeing her ex-stepmother. They might never be best friends, but Beth had matured enough to accept that her father's happiness was far more important.

Rick had bought Beth some memory books so she could record Riley's milestones, and Granny had chosen some tiny dresses and sleepers. Granny loved the locket, and Rick put on his new sweater right away.

Riley slept through most of the celebrations as she was passed from lap to lap to be cuddled and held. She was the favorite present that Christmas—the tiny girl who'd stolen all their hearts.

Rick held his granddaughter now, snuggled up against his chest, when there was a knock at the door. Neighbors, no doubt. Beth went to answer it, and when she opened the door, she saw Danny standing there, his son in front of him.

"Merry Christmas," Luke said.

"Merry Christmas, Luke." Beth stepped back to let them in, and as Danny passed her, his dark gaze met hers, and her heart sped up in her chest. Why couldn't she turn off her emotions for this man? But she found herself feeling relieved that he was here...

"Daniel!" A smile split across Granny's face. "I am so glad you've come! Should I take Luke to the kitchen—"

"No, no..." Danny licked his lips, then his gaze dropped down to Beth again. "Luke's a part of this, too. Could we talk, Beth?"

She nodded, and Danny and Luke took off their boots. Luke crossed the living room to look at the baby in Rick's arms, and Danny reached forward to tuck a tendril behind Beth's ear.

"I love you," he said softly.

"Danny—" Love wasn't the problem, here. If love were all they needed, she had enough to cover the both of them.

"Beth, hear me out," he pleaded. "I've had to accept the fact that I'm not going to stop loving you. I'm stuck. But I think there's hope for us."

"Is there?" If only he could be right, but she didn't see how. They'd been through this before.

"You need to know that I won't hide anything from you again," he said. "So here's what I've got."

He pulled a file folder out of his jacket and handed it to her. Beth turned it over in her hands. "Loving you isn't the problem, Danny... I love Luke, too. He's a sweetheart...but life gets hard."

"Open it," he said.

Beth opened the file and looked down on what looked like some banking documents and a sheet of paper with a phone number and a Vancouver address.

"That's it—all of it," he said. "That's Lana's

contact information, and that's all my banking info. No more surprises. You can see what debt I've got, what assets… You can contact Lana anytime you feel is necessary. I don't have anything else hidden away, Beth, except for this love for you that I just can't seem to get over. So I'm going to take Granny's advice and recognize when I'm beat."

"Danny—"

"Beth, you're going to mess up," he went on. "We've both made mistakes, and I think you're scared that any more in the future will affect the kids."

Beth was silent. She was afraid of that… and she was afraid that whatever challenges arose would prove too much for them if Danny clammed up and stopped talking.

"I'll mess up, too," he went on. "So will the kids. We'll all mess up, probably on a regular basis. So here's what I can offer you. We'll forgive you."

Beth blinked, searching his face for the punch line. "What?"

"I'm serious," he said. "Luke messed up big-time last night, and you know what I did? I forgave him. Because he's my son, and I love him. And I've messed up with him before, and Luke forgave me. Like when I yell at him, or he gets in trouble for something he didn't do. Mistakes happen—a whole lot. Welcome to being a parent, Beth."

"It'll be complicated sometimes," she said. "I'll need you to level with me—about everything!"

"Can you love us?" Danny asked.

"Of course!" A tear escaped and trickled down her cheek.

"I can love you, too," Luke added from across the room.

"And if I mess up, Luke?" she asked, turning toward the boy. "If you think I'm horribly unfair?"

Luke shrugged. "I can forgive you for stuff."

"Here's the thing, Beth," Danny said. "I'm going to love you for the rest of my life, whether you marry me or not. But I want to be a family. I want to face all of these hurdles together—you and me. And I want to love our kids and give it our best shot. I want you to be my wife, and I want you to be Luke's mom."

"You want—" She didn't dare finish the sentence.

"To marry you," Danny concluded. "Yes."

She stood there, his words washing over her, and she longed to say yes.

"Granny isn't a huge fan of original vows," Danny said with a small smile. "But here are mine—I'll love you no matter what. I'll tell you everything. There will be no secrets, and I'll stand by you whatever comes our way. I'll be yours, Beth. And that starts now—not at a wedding."

"What do you think, Luke?" Beth asked, looking back to the boy whose glistening eyes were now fixed on them. "Could you love a baby sister?"

"Yeah!" Luke grinned. "I'd take him, too!" The boy hooked a thumb toward Rick, and Beth couldn't help laughing.

Beth turned back to Danny, and he looked at her expectantly.

"Yes?" he whispered hopefully.

"Yes."

Danny's lips came down onto hers and he slid his arms around her, pulling her closer. His hands moved up to her face, and then he broke off the kiss and reached into his pocket. Between his fingers he held a tiny ring—but she recognized it immediately. It was the ring he'd proposed with six years ago.

"Danny—" Her breath caught. "You still have it?"

"It wasn't worth much to anyone else," he said with a shrug. "And I'll get you a better one, but I hoped that for now—"

"No!" Beth held out her hand, and her fingers trembled. "I want this one! It's ours."

Danny slid the ring onto her finger once more. It was small—just a tiny diamond on a simple band, but it was perfect.

"I'm not sure if I should have consulted with you first, sir," Danny said, shooting Rick a wry smile. "But I didn't want to take any chances."

Rick's expression remained grim, and he came forward to shake Danny's hand, the other hand holding Riley against his shoulder. "If you break her heart—"

"I won't, sir." Danny met Rick's gaze. "I'll take good care of them. That's a promise."

Luke slid between them, and Beth bent down to give the boy a hug. This was her family—she could hardly believe it… Would her love be enough for them all? She could give it her best shot—open her heart and love them all so hard that she'd never have regrets.

But looking up into Danny's dark gaze—the tenderness there, the depth of love—she felt a settling, a peacefulness.

"I love you, Beth," Danny said quietly.

"I love you, too."

He kissed her once more, then Danny turned to Rick.

"Mind if I hold her?" Danny asked hopefully. Rick passed Riley into his arms, and Danny looked down into her tiny face. He brushed the back of one finger down her hand, then pressed his lips to her forehead. He closed his eyes, breathing her in, then he opened them and met Beth's gaze.

"Yep," Danny said, his voice tight with emotion. "I can do this, Beth. This is my little girl."

Danny exhaled a sigh that sounded like relief, and she understood all too well. It was a risk—love always was—but it was a relief to simply take the leap. She loved him—she loved *them*.

This was home.

EPILOGUE

BETH STOOD IN the kitchen of what used to be Danny's house but now was theirs. She held a small bowl of cooked sweet potato, and she was mashing it with a fork. Riley was in the high chair, slapping her hands against the plastic tray. This would be her first try with solid food—a big day! But Beth had something else she needed to do today, too.

Outside, spring was in full swing, and Luke was digging a hole in the garden. He'd been playing out there all morning in a sunny patch where the snow had melted. He was mining, he said. Looking for diamonds. Beth squeezed the phone receiver between her cheek and her shoulder as she mashed the sweet potato.

"Lana, here's the thing," she said, turning her attention back to her conversation. "Luke needs to know you."

"I'm not much of a mom," Lana replied, her voice low.

"But you're *his* mom," Beth replied. "And I can't take your place. I'm here, too, and I adore him, but that doesn't erase you. I'm here every day and I always will be. I take care of his needs and keep him safe. I love him with all my heart, but that doesn't mean he'll ever stop wanting to know *you*."

"What do you want from me?" Lana asked uncertainly.

"Danny and I will pay for a week in a hotel here in North Fork," Beth said. "We want you to come and visit your son."

"And you'd be fine with that?" Lana asked, her tone slightly less respectful. "You'd be okay with Daniel and me spending time with our son together?"

Lana was trying to scare her, but it wasn't going to work. There was no chance that Danny would stop loving Beth, and she knew that. She had his heart—this wasn't about their relationship or about her security.

"I'll be here," Beth replied evenly. "I'm a part of this family, too, you know. And no, I'm not threatened. This isn't about you or me, Lana. This isn't about turf. This is about

Luke and what he needs. He's been asking to meet you, and I want to make that possible."

"You want me to come visit?" Lana repeated dubiously.

"Please." Beth softened her tone. "Luke loves you and wants to know you."

Lana was silent for a moment, then she sighed. "I'll think about it. I'll call you back."

"Okay," Beth replied. "That sounds good. I'll talk to you later."

As Beth hung up, she saw movement in the doorway, and she turned to see Danny standing there, his dark gaze locked on her. His broad shoulders filled the doorway, and she was struck anew by just how good-looking he was.

"That right there," he said gruffly. "That's why I married you."

Beth shrugged weakly. "She didn't promise anything."

"But you're trying," Danny replied. "And it means the world to Luke."

Danny crossed the room and bent to catch her lips with his. Then he took the bowl of mashed sweet potatoes from her.

"Mind if I do the honors?" he asked.

Beth laughed. "Sure."

Luke and what he needs. He's been asking to meet you, and I want to make that possible."

"You want me to come visit?" Lana repeated dubiously.

"Please." Beth softened her tone. "Luke loves you and wants to know you."

Lana was silent for a moment, then she sighed. "I'll think about it. I'll call you back."

"Okay," Beth replied. "That sounds good. I'll talk to you later."

As Beth hung up, she saw movement in the doorway, and she turned to see Danny standing there, his dark gaze locked on her. His broad shoulders filled the doorway, and she was struck anew by just how good-looking he was.

"That right there," he said gruffly. "That's why I married you."

Beth shrugged weakly. "She didn't promise anything."

"But you're trying," Danny replied. "And it means the world to Luke."

Danny crossed the room and bent to catch her lips with his. Then he took the bowl of mashed sweet potatoes from her.

"Mind if I do the honors?" he asked.

Beth laughed. "Sure."

Danny grabbed a baby spoon and crouched in front of the high chair.

"Oh, this looks so delicious," Danny said enthusiastically, scooping a tiny bit on the end of the spoon and popping it into Riley's mouth. Her eyes opened in surprise, and father and daughter stared at each other while Riley spit the orange dribble back out.

"No?" Danny looked hurt. "You sure?"

He tried again, and Beth laughed as Riley spat it out once more. Maybe sweet potatoes weren't going to be a favorite. They'd try something else. Beth slid her arms around her husband's neck and leaned her cheek against his hair.

They were the Brockwoods, and they might not be the perfect family, Beth knew, but they were patched together with love. It filled the gaps. It smoothed over the rough patches, and it made all the difference.

* * * * *

*If you enjoyed this story,
check out Patricia Johns's earlier stories
from Harlequin Heartwarming,
A BAXTER'S REDEMPTION
and
THE RUNAWAY BRIDE.*

And look for her next book in 2018!